PARANORMAL
OBJECT STORIES

FROM AMAZON BESTSELLING AUTHOR
OF PARANORMAL MORGUE STORIES

EVE S EVANS

ALSO
—BY—
EVE S EVANS

Fiction:

The Haunting of Hartley House
Hartley House Homecoming
The Haunting of Crow House
The Haunting of Redburn Manor
Origins
Beneath The Water
Mistletoe Magic
The Haunting of Lila Lamm
Frost Falls

Anthologies:

True Ghost Stories of First Responders
Haunted Asylums
Holiday Hauntings
Shadow People
Chilling Ghost Stories
Haunted Hotels
Haunted Hospitals
Haunted Objects
Paranormal Pets
Haunted on Vacation
Haunted Murder Houses
Haunted Lakes
Supernatural 911 Calls
Demonic Hauntings
When I Died

Don't forget to join my email newsletter! I do several "mystery box" giveaways each year!

(You can also find the link in my bio on instagram: eves.evansauthor)

Newsletter Signup (mailchi.mp)

Giveaways include: Bookmarks, autographed paperbacks, book lover merch, horror merch, paranormal merch and much more!

— Eve

The contents of this book have been curated from legends and tales spanning across the globe, and may include fictional stories that have been passed down for generations. While the aim is to present authentic ghost stories, some may be rooted more in mythology or folklore.

REAL GHOST STORY

Shadowed Heritage

REAL GHOST
STORY

Shadowed Heritage

The ring had been a prized heirloom, passed down through my husband's family for generations. I hadn't even known about it until the wedding. When my husband and I had first gotten engaged, he'd picked out a beautiful diamond ring for me that I had quickly grown to love.

At the wedding, however, his family presented me with the wedding ring as a gift, and I had been so surprised and honored to receive such a beautiful heirloom that I ended up replacing the diamond ring with the gold band instead.

After the wedding, my husband and I moved into a new house in a new city, excited for our new lives to begin together.

It wasn't long, however, before things started to happen.

Strange things. Things I couldn't immediately explain with rational thought.

A few weeks after moving into the house, I got up in the middle of the night to go to the bathroom. My husband, Jake, was still fast asleep, snoring quietly in bed, so I tiptoed into the ensuite and shut the door behind me.

The tiles were ice-cold, and there was a strange chill in the air that was unbefitting for the middle of summer. As soon as I closed the door behind me, I was pitched into darkness, fumbling blindly for the light switch.

Instead of the plastic switch, my fingers brushed something cold and *soft,* and I withdrew with a short gasp, blinking rapidly to see in the dark.

There was nothing there, so I tried again, my fingers flipping the switch and filtering light into the room.

The lights buzzed and dimmed, and in that fraction of a second as the shadows dispersed, I thought I glimpsed something in the mirror. Something white standing right beside me.

I stumbled away and looked between the mirror and the room, but there was nothing there.

I figured I must have imagined it, and tried to brush it from my mind. I was still a little stressed from the move, so I chalked it down to simply being tired.

Only, that wasn't the last time I glimpsed that strange white figure in the mirror.

A few days later, while I was in the house alone, I was in the middle of doing some laundry when I heard the door creak open behind me. I turned around with a frown, wondering if Jake had come home early, but there was nobody there.

Assuming the breeze must have blown it open, I went to close it when I saw something white flit around the corner in front of me, like the beat of a moth's wing.

The air around me suddenly went very cold, and my mouth went dry.

Despite the trepidation in my chest, I stepped out of the room and peered around the corner. A shadow snagged the edges of my vision, but when I turned to look at it, there was nothing there.

I wanted to tell myself that I was just being silly, and that I was imagining it, but for it to happen twice was odd. It felt like more than a coincidence.

Tensions began to rise during this time too, between Jake and I. I had known from the start that marriage wasn't easy, but I had never known Jake and I to fight like this. Everything he did seemed to rattle my nerves and make me irritated for no reason, and he seemed to get upset over the smallest things I did too.

We'd been living together for years before we got married, so it seemed odd that the problems would suddenly start now.

About two months after moving in, Jake and I had a particularly bad fight, and he left the house to go and clear his head. I was in the house alone, nursing my own wounds and trying to dispel the bitterness I was feeling for no reason, when I heard a door creak open upstairs.

The house wasn't very old, and I had no windows open at the time, so I found it odd straight away. I wondered if Jake had come back without me realization, but when I glanced outside, his car was still gone.

Curious and unnerved, I grabbed a knife from the kitchen and went upstairs to check it out.

The carpet muffled my footsteps, but I was breathing loud enough that I could hear it, my pulse drowning out the silence.

"Hello? Is there someone up here?" I called, noticing that the door to the bedroom was sitting wide-open. I never left doors open like that. Ajar, perhaps, but not gaping open, enough to see the whole frame of the room.

I peeked inside, but there was nobody there. I thought I was just overthinking things again, but then the air turned cold enough that I could see my breath in front of me, and I knew *that* wasn't normal.

Feeling suddenly like I wasn't alone, I dialed Jake's number on my phone. When he didn't answer, I sent him a text to come home, but for some reason, the message wouldn't send, so I gave up.

I knew that *something* was going on, but I didn't know what. The house was like any other house, and it had no history of any tragic deaths, so there was no reason it would be haunted (not that I was even sure I believed in ghosts).

Whatever was causing this, it wasn't the house. It was something else.

I put the pieces together slowly.

Everything that had happened had coincided with moving into this house. But also, our wedding. None of this discord between Jake and I had manifested until the wedding either. At first I thought that perhaps that was just the curse of married couples, but there was something unnatural about it. Like some external force was driving the tensions up between us.

Then, a couple of months after the wedding, I saw her.

It was in the middle of the night, when I'd gotten up to get a drink from downstairs. I stood at the sink, filling a glass with water from the tap, when I saw movement out of the corner of my eye. I twisted off the faucet and looked up, my eyes finding hers in the reflection of the window.

A woman, pale as a corpse, in a rotten wedding dress. She was standing behind me, her face obscured by the netted veil she wore, but I saw the faint glint of eyes, dark and sunken, watching me.

I stared at her, as if in a trance, hardly knowing if she was real or not.

Then I felt her breath on my neck, ice-cold, and reality came rushing back to me.

I screamed, the glass of water slipping between my fingers and shattering on the kitchen floor.

Jake came rushing downstairs and switched on the light, and she disappeared, as if she were no more than a figment of my imagination.

"What's wrong? What happened?" He said, taking in my horrified expression, the broken glass at my feet, the water seeping along the tiles.

I stuttered, but couldn't find the words to answer him, knowing he wouldn't believe me if I told him the truth.

"I-I'm sorry," I finally said once my heart had calmed down, my pulse no longer thudding in my ears. "I thought I saw something."

Jake frowned, but he didn't ask any more questions, which I was grateful for. A fatigued expression crossed his face. "Why don't you head back to bed? I'll get this cleaned up."

I hesitated. "No, it's my mess," I said, but I could tell he was getting annoyed, so I kept quiet and went back to bed, still trying to get the imagine of the woman out of my mind.

Had she been real? Why was she wearing a wedding dress?

It was later that night, when I was dreaming about what I saw, that I remembered something else. Something I had seen the woman wearing when she was standing behind me. For just a second, I had glimpsed her hand--her long, pale fingers. And the wedding band she was wearing. Gold. Identical to the one I had been given by my husband's family.

At first I thought it was just my mind making connections where there were none, but the more I considered it, the more sense it made. I was being haunted by the phantom of a bride, and none of it had started until the wedding--until the day I got that ring.

The next day, after Jake had left for work, I decided to do some research. The wedding band had a small imprint on the inside, a hallmark, that allowed me to trace it's history. From what I could gather, the ring had been in my husband's family for decades, but the first ever record of it was from 1963. I did some more digging into the family's history, and discovered that in September 1963, one Mary Ingleson was jilted at the altar on her wedding day, and took her revenge by cursing my husband's family before brutally killing herself.

That woman that I had been seeing... was that Mary? Was she still haunting my husband's family through the ring, and now they had passed that curse on to me?

I didn't know if I had all the facts straight, but it seemed to make sense. It explained why my husband and I were having difficulties with our marriage, if Mary had been jilted by her own lover.

I glanced down at the wedding band, turning it over in my hand. If this was the cause of all the misfortune, it only made sense to destroy the ring, or at least get rid of it.

But what if that only broke mine and Jake's relationship even more? It had belonged to his family, after all, and it didn't feel right to just throw it away.

Swallowing hard, I put the ring away in a drawer, and hoped that maybe the ghost of Mary would somehow find the ability to move on.

REAL GHOST STORY

Haunting Melody

REAL GHOST STORY

Haunting Melody

The morning was dull and overcast as I wheeled my bike down the street of an unfamiliar neighborhood.

I'd been on my way to the library when a piece of unseen glass had punctured the tire of my bike and sent all the air gushing out like a popped balloon, leaving me stranded in the middle of nowhere.

I considered calling my mom for a ride home, but I figured she'd probably be busy, so instead I started wheeling it down the street, despairing over how much it would cost to replace the tire.

The neighborhood was in a more run-down part of town, where the houses were made of dark brick and there were trash bags sitting out on the corners, unclaimed.

The wind picked up, and an empty soda can rattled against the gutters, making me jump.

I wanted to get out of there quickly, so I hurried my pace, the bike creaking and hissing as it bumped over the pavement.

At the end of the street, I saw the sign for a garage sale, pointing down the next road. At first, I ignored it, thinking I'd rather not stick around. But when I turned the corner and saw the tables full of stuff, I hesitated. Maybe I could find a new tire there. It seemed unlikely, but it didn't hurt to have a look. It would be way cheaper than buying something new at a repair shop.

There were a couple of other people taking a look too, which eased some of my trepidation, so I went over, leaving my bike tied to a lamppost.

The tables were mostly full of junk. Old tools and magazines and some old, stained furniture. No bicycle tires. But there was *something* that caught my eye.

It was a music box. I used to love music boxes when I was a kid, and I remember owning a few different ones before I lost interest and my mom gave them all away.

But something about this one drew me to it, and I found it in my hand before I could help it.

"You've got a good eye," a voice said near my ear, and I gave a start, almost dropping the beautiful silver-edged box. The old woman chuckled. "Sorry, didn't mean to scare you, lass."

I shook my head. "You didn't scare me," I muttered, despite my heart racing in my chest.

Swallowing, I put the music box back down. I doubted I'd have enough for it anyway. I only had a couple of bucks in my pockets to get a drink at the library.

"Not interested?" She crooned.

"Too expensive," I amended.

The old woman laughed. "How much do you have?"

I turned out my pockets, showing her. "Not enough."

"It's enough for me," she said. "Go on, take it."

"Are you sure?" The woman nodded, so I handed her the money and picked up the box again, cradling it against my chest. "Thank you."

The woman walked away, chuckling, and I went to grab my bike, tucking the music box safely into the basket as I wheeled it back home.

That night, I played the music box for the first time. It was one of the ones where you could see the mechanisms turning inside like clockwork as it played. The tune was slow and haunting and beautiful, and as I listened to it, I could feel myself growing drowsy, almost like it was luring me into a trance.

I quickly sobered, however, when I heard something thud in my room, and glanced around.

The light was on but dim, and shadows encroached in the corners of the room as dusk fell outside. It took me a moment to place where the noise had come from.

A couple of the books on my desk shelf had fallen off, and now lay splayed on the floor, the spines cracked.

Setting down the music box, I climbed off the bed and went over to pick them up. Why had they fallen over so suddenly? I hadn't touched any of these books in a while, so it wasn't like they had been loose or balancing on the edge. They had been firmly stuffed inside the shelf.

Behind me, the music box abruptly stopped playing, and a faint chill touched my neck.

Had the room always been this cold?

I hastily returned the books to the shelf, making sure they were wedged in there, and went back to the box, twisting the dial to play the tune again.

I fell asleep with the strange melody on my mind.

The next day, I woke late. It was Sunday, so I spent the morning lazing around before remembering the music box, and what had happened last night. This time, the books had stayed on the shelf, and I breathed a sigh of relief. It must have just been a weird coincidence.

I picked up the music box from where I had left it on my bedside table, and began to play it again, admiring the way all the mechanisms moved in sync to produce the melody.

As I was listening to it in the quiet of my room, I heard the soft pad of footsteps moving along the hallway outside my room. I would have just thought it was my mom, but these sounded *heavy* somehow, not at all like her soft shuffle.

Curious, I set the box down and went to see if she was out there.

Cracking open the door, I looked out, and found the hallway empty. A shiver of trepidation ran along the back of my neck.

When I listened closely, I could hear water running in the bathroom down the hall. If mom was taking a shower, then who had I heard walking past my room?

Swallowing back the lump in my throat, I closed the door again and went to turn the music box off, no longer feeling the desire to listen to its tune.

I was back at school the next day, so I didn't get chance to play, or even think about, the music box until I got home.

The second I opened the door to my bedroom, I could hear it playing, its haunting melody swirling around the room like a damp autumn breeze. I looked inside, but there was nobody in there.

Who had set it off?

I walked over to the box and picked it up, and it stopped suddenly, as if my touch had silenced it.

Behind me, I heard the soft pad of footsteps, and gave a start. Turning round, I saw my mom standing in the doorway. Her eyes fell on the music box in my hand.

"Oh, sorry, I was listening to it before you came home," she explained, but somehow, it didn't help the shiver of unease that rooted itself in my chest. "It's beautiful."

I simply nodded, setting it back down. "Yeah."

I didn't play the music box for the rest of the evening, but my gaze kept being drawn towards it, like something was prompting me to go and turn it on. But I didn't.

That night, I woke up to the soft sound of music playing in my room.

I woke slowly, sleep threatening to drag me back under, until I realized what I was hearing.

I bolted up in bed, wide-awake, and blinked. The music box was playing on my bedside table. I knew I hadn't touched it in my sleep, because my hands had been under my pillow.

Was it playing on its own?

I let out a slow, shaky breath, looking around.

The darkness felt thicker than usual, and I got the strange, creeping feeling that I was not alone. There was someone--or something--in my room, lurking in the shadows.

My heart thudded dully in my ears as I reached past the music box, for the lamp. Just as my fingers brushed the switch, I heard something in the dark that made me draw my hand back, terrified.

A whisper.

It sounded like it had said my name, but I couldn't be sure. My pulse was too loud in my ears for me to have heard it properly.

The music box stopped playing suddenly, and I finally got the courage to switch the light on.

Out of the corner of my eye, I thought I saw a shadow lingering in the corner, but when I looked, it was gone. The rest of the room was empty, still. Nothing there.

I didn't turn the light off for the rest of the night, and the music box didn't make a sound.

I was exhausted by the time dawn broke, but it didn't stop me from climbing out of bed, grabbing the music box, and taking it downstairs to toss it in the trash.

As beautiful as the tune it played was, I couldn't spend every night cowering in fear for what lurked in the shadows.

REAL GHOST STORY

Haunted Between the Seams

REAL GHOST STORY

Haunted Between
The Seams

I was eight years old when my twin sister died.

We'd been playing outside, like we always did, chasing each other around the garden and throwing a bouncy ball between us, because we liked the way the sun bounced off its shiny plastic surface.

Our mom had gone inside to answer a phone call, leaving us outside alone. It had taken no more than five minutes.

My sister had accidentally missed the ball, and it had gone rolling through the open fence, out onto the road. With a grin, she'd told me that she would go and fetch it, that she would be right back.

Only, she never did come back.

I'd heard the skid of brakes, and the heart-wrenching scream, and it felt like the ground had completely give way beneath me, though at the time, I didn't know why.

I didn't really know what had happened (my mom refused to tell me the truth). All I knew was that my twin--my best friend--was never coming back to me. We would never play together again.

I had a difficult time moving on after that. I would sit in the garden and wait for her to come back, even though some part of me knew that it was silly, because she was gone. I knew what death meant, but I refused to accept it.

To help me cope with the grief, my mom gave me my sister's teddy bear. She'd had it for years, since she was very young, and it was getting a little threadbare in places. One of the black button-eyes had even come loose and was hanging on mostly by a thin thread, but it had still been her favourite.

For me, it was the only piece of her that I had left. It even still smelled like her, so I kept hold of it like it was the only thing that mattered.

It didn't take long, however, for things to get weird.

A couple of nights after my mom had given me the bear, I woke up in the middle of the night to what sounded like crying. At first I thought it was my mom, because I'd heard her a few times crying alone in her bedroom after my twin had passed away. But something about this was different.

I got up and turned on a light. The crying was definitely coming from somewhere inside my room.

Clutching onto my sister's teddy bear, I climbed out of bed and went over to the closet. When I put my ear against the wood, the crying was louder. It was coming from inside the closet.

I didn't really understand what was happening. Why was someone crying in my closet?

I was scared, but also curious, so I reached for the handle and pulled it open slowly.

As soon as I opened the door, the crying stopped. Everything went quiet, still. A shiver touched my neck, even though it was a warm July night.

I looked inside the closet, but couldn't see anything, so I closed the doors and went back to bed, thinking nothing more of it.

A few nights later, I woke up again. This time, it wasn't the sound of crying that had pulled me from my sleep, but something else.

Something more strange, and more terrifying.

It sounded like someone was scratching at the wall behind my bed. Like long nails, tearing through the wallpaper, grating over the plaster beneath.

I lay frozen in bed, too scared to move, too scared to even breath, feeling like I wasn't alone but being too terrified to look.

My sister's teddy lay clutched in my arms, and I squeezed it even tighter, expecting it to bring me comfort.

Instead, the noises only seemed to get worse, getting louder, closer. I felt like something was moving across the room, coming towards me.

I wanted to burrow under the covers and pretend there was nothing there, but instead, I managed to blink open an eye and take a look around the room.

For just a moment, I thought I saw someone standing there. A figure, darker than the shadows, standing near the bed, watching me.

I gasped, my blood running cold, but then it was gone.

I looked down at the teddy in my arms, at its dark button eyes, and felt a prickle of fear. Somehow, it didn't seem so comforting anymore.

I put the bear at the end of the bed where I couldn't see it, and finally, the noises stopped. The air seemed to grow lighter again, like whatever had been here had left.

I left the bear on the end of the bed for the rest of the night, and when I woke up the next morning, it had fallen to the floor.

It didn't take me long to realize that these strange and creepy things had started after my mom had given me my sister's teddy bear. Was the toy causing it? Or was it something else?

I didn't have the answers, nor did I really know how to get them, so I left things as they were, hoping it would stop.

It didn't.

On the nights when I took the teddy bear to bed with me, something strange would always happen. Sometimes it would be nothing more than a whisper in the dark, or a cold patch of air in the room that didn't seem to go. But sometimes, I would wake up and see shadows moving around my room, or hear that strange sobbing coming from the closet.

I began to learn that not having the bear with me made it stop, but somehow, I couldn't let it go. The teddy was the only thing I had left of my sister, and despite the creepy things that seemed to happen when it was near me, my grief was stronger, and it begged me not to get rid of the bear.

So I kept it, and over time, I got used to the strange happenings.

It wasn't until a few years later, when I was older and had a better understanding of life and death, that I considered the possibility the teddy bear was haunted by my sister. Maybe all these strange occurrences had merely been her way of trying to communicate from beyond the veil. But who could really say for certain?

REAL GHOST STORY

Hane-Me-Down

REAL GHOST STORY

Hand-Me-Down

I had been given the dress as a hand-me-down from my fiancé's mother. It was a beautiful dress, with a full-skirted white satin gown and white lace sleeves. It was a tradition in their family to hand it down to the new generation, and I had felt honored to be given the opportunity to be part of the family in this way.

The first time I tried it on was when I went to the local seamstress to have the fit altered.

I was alone in the room while I was putting it on, but one of the ladies came in to help me fasten it up.

As she was adjusting some of the edges and making sure it properly fastened, I was overcome with an abrupt feeling of sadness. It was almost suffocating, to the point where I couldn't breathe for all the emotion welling in my chest.

The seamstress thought I was simply being overwhelmed by the dress, but it had nothing to do with that. I could barely even pay attention to what I looked like because I was feeling so *sad,* and I couldn't figure out why.

I told her that I was fine, and that she could go ahead with measuring and adjusting the dress. After a while, the sadness faded, but I still felt strange, and I couldn't shake away the feeling that something was wrong with me.

It was only after I had taken the dress off that I felt perfectly fine again, like nothing had happened. I figured that maybe the seamstress was right, and that I was simply feeling emotional because I was finally getting married.

I thought nothing of it until a few nights later, when I woke up in the middle of the night.

My husband was still asleep, and the room was pitch-black, barely illuminated by the sickle-shaped moon outside.

Nothing seemed to have woken me up, so I turned around to go back to sleep. And that's when I saw it. Someone standing at the foot of the bed. It was only for a second, a brief glimpse in the darkness, but I was certain there was someone there.

The shadows had covered most of it, but I had glimpsed pale, glinting eyes, and the clear silhouette of a woman's face.

I sat up and looked around the room, but I couldn't see it anymore, and I had to wonder if I had simply imagined it.

My husband woke up then, asking if something was wrong, but I just shook my head and told him to go back to sleep. I doubt he'd believe me if I told him I saw someone in the room, so I kept it to myself and tried to fall back asleep, though it evaded me for the rest of the night.

The same thing happened a few nights later, only this time, I heard her too. I woke up to the sound of someone whispering in the room, and when I looked up, she was there, just standing at the foot of the bed, like some haunting specter.

Ice-cold dread settled in the pit of my stomach because, this time, I knew I wasn't imagining it. The whispers faded, but she stayed where she was, watching me with those pale, sunken eyes.

I reached blindly across the bed to shake my husband awake, without taking my eyes of the shadowy figure standing in our room. She didn't move.

My husband groaned quietly as I shook him awake, sweat dribbling down the back of my neck.

Only, when he finally woke up, the woman was already gone, disappearing like a shadow into the corners of the room.

I switched on a light and looked around, but she was nowhere to be seen.

Nothing but a phantom.

I didn't know who this woman was, or what she wanted, but it wasn't the last I saw of her.

I was driving to work one morning when I glanced up to the rear view mirror and the blood drained from my face.

Someone was sitting in the back seat of the car.

It was what could only be described as a pale, almost-translucent looking figure, and I blinked rapidly to make sure it wasn't just a trick of the light, my heart racing madly in my chest.

I flicked my gaze back to the road and pulled to a stop at a traffic light, then twisted in my seat to look at the back seat. There was nothing there. I looked again into the mirror, but the back of the car was now empty. The figure was gone.

The lights changed, and I hit the accelerator, trying not to panic about what I had just seen.

Maybe it was just the way the light was shining through the windows, making me see something that wasn't really there.

But just as the thought crossed my mind, I felt a cold breath touch the back of my neck, and heard a female voice whisper my name.

I almost hit the breaks in my panic, but I managed to stay calm, my palms sweaty as I clicked on the indicator and pulled the car to the side of the road, cutting the engine.

My heart pounded in my chest, and for a second, I wondered if I was going crazy. These things that I was seeing, and hearing. Was it all just in my head? I'd been stressed lately because of the wedding, but I didn't expect it to manifest like this.

With trembling hands, I called my fiancé. I hadn't told him about the other incidences, but I couldn't hide it from him anymore. I had to tell *someone.*

I told him what had happened in the car, and even as I said it out loud, I knew how ridiculous it sounded. Of course he wasn't going to believe me. I wasn't even sure if I believed myself.

"Lisa, I... I don't really know what you want me to say," he said quietly, and I felt my chest clench.

"I know it sounds crazy," I finally said, shaking my head. "I'm sorry. Maybe I'm just feeling the pressure lately. I'd better get to work." I hung up before he could say anything else, took a few deep, shaky breaths, and re-joined the flow of traffic. On the way to work, I kept glancing up at the rear-view, but the figure never returned, and gradually I forgot all about it.

In the weeks leading up to the wedding, things got worse.

The night after I'd gone to another fitting of the wedding dress, I had a nightmare.

At the time, it had felt so real that I hadn't even realized it was just a dream.

In the dream, I woke up to the sound of glass shattering downstairs. There was a shape in the bed next to me that I assumed was my fiancé, but instead of waking him up, I got up and opened the door, listening for anything else.

Downstairs, I could hear footsteps. For some reason, I felt compelled to go and see what it was, so I left the safety of the bedroom and padded down the stairs into the kitchen. I turned the corner, and froze.

There was someone standing there, holding a knife. I couldn't see who it was. It was nothing more than a shadow, tall and featureless, but I knew he was going to hurt me.

He lunged for me with the knife, and I turned and ran, screaming, but the darkness seemed to thicken around me, dragging me back towards him, no matter how hard I tried to run away.

The shadowy figure managed to grab my leg and drag me backwards, and that was when I woke up, sweat pouring down my forehead, panting heavily.

My fiancé woke up and tried to calm me down, but every shadow in the room terrified me, and I couldn't sleep for the rest of the night.

A few days later, I was cooking in the kitchen. It was later than usual, and it was already getting dark outside, shadows accumulating around the edges of the room, despite all the lights being on.

I had vegetables simmering in a pan on the stove, and turned round to switch off the gas and lift the pan off the cooker.

As I was doing this, something made me glance up, and my heart lurched into my stomach. A face was peering through the window in front of me. It was a woman, with brown hair and almond eyes, and as soon as she saw me, she pulled away and melted back into the night.

I screamed, almost dropping the pan. Managing to get it safely back on the stove, I ran to the back door and threw it open, looking out into the night.

There was nobody there. The woman had already gone.

My fiancé came rushing downstairs to see what was wrong, and found me on the kitchen floor with my head in my hands.

"I think I'm going crazy," I told him. "I keep seeing things. Things I don't understand."

He pulled me into his arms and held me until I calmed down, and was rational enough again to talk about what had happened.

"This woman... is it the same one every time?"

I bit my lip, then shook my head. "I don't know. I don't think so. I think they might be different."

"When did it start?" He asked, surprisingly calm about everything. I couldn't tell if he believed me, but at least he was trying to understand it and not just calling me crazy.

I stayed quiet for a while, trying to recall when all the strange things had started happening. There was only one thing I could think of that had been notable. "The wedding dress. Everything started after I tried on the wedding dress."

He pursed his lips. "It's been in my family for a long time," he told me, his tone ruminative. "Maybe my mom knows more about it. Why don't you give her a call? I'll sort the rest of dinner out."

I nodded and headed upstairs to call my fiancé's mom. We decided to meet the next day so that she could tell me a bit more about the dress, and I hoped that I would somehow find out why I was seeing the things that I was.

She came round to the house the following morning, toting a photo album in her arms. My fiancé was at work, so I made tea for the two of us and we sat down in the living room. I decided not to tell her about the figures I had been seeing just yet, and instead asked her to tell me about the dress she had given me.

The dress had been in her family for generations, passing down to each new bride on their wedding day. Over the years, it had been altered and changed, as if each new thread and lace held the history of each new bride.

"I have a photo," she told me, bringing out the album, "of the very first bride to wear the dress. Although it's changed, it's still recognizable."

I felt a shiver of unease before she even showed me the photo, and when she did, it was like all the breath had been stolen from my lungs.

The woman in the photo was the same woman I had seen standing at my window last night.

"These are the other brides, too," she continued, flipping through the album of wedding photos. Each woman wore the same dress that I now owned. I recognized a few more of the women as those I had seen standing in my room, and sitting in the back of my car.

"What happened to them all?"

She gave me a curious look. "Well, most of them have already passed away," she said. "Some of them met rather unfortunate ends. One died in a car crash, and another was murdered during a home invasion."

For a moment, it felt like the floor was tilting under my feet, and I had to grip the couch's cushions to keep me steady.

"Are you alright, love? You've gone a bit pale," she said, closing the photo album.

"I'm fine. Things just... make a lot more sense now," I said, without clarifying.

The wedding dress was the source of all these strange apparitions after all. Since I had inherited the dress, I was seeing all the past brides who had passed away while owning it in the past.

With the wedding only a couple of weeks away, I could only hope that once it was over, the spirits of the dress' previous brides would eventually leave me alone.

REAL GHOST STORY

Haunted But Cherished

REAL GHOST STORY

Haunted But Cherished

A few weeks after my grandma passed away, I inherited an old vase from the flower shop she used to own.

My mom brought it home, wrapped in dozens of pieces of bubble wrap and stored safely in a cardboard box, with my name on a label on the front.

I'd never seen the vase before, and thought it odd that my grandma had chosen me specifically to inherit it, given I'd never really shown an interest in vases or flowers in the past.

Still, I kept it in honour of my grandma's memory, and displayed it proudly in my home, on a shelf in my office.

My husband was away working a lot, so I was in the house alone a lot of the time, since I worked freelance from a home office. I'd gotten used to being in the house alone, and most of the time it didn't bother me.

But about a month after my grandma's funeral, I started getting the odd feeling that I wasn't alone. It can only really be described as an instinctual feeling; a strange flutter in my chest, and a tighten of my stomach, like my body knew something was wrong.

I was home alone one afternoon, working in my office, when that same feeling washed over me, stronger than before. All the hairs on the back of my neck stood on end, and a shiver worked its way down my back, making goosebumps prickle my skin.

I stopped what I was doing and turned to look around the room.

The first thing I noticed was that the door was shut.

I always kept it open when I worked in the office, so that I could hear if anyone was at the door, or if the phone rang. I distinctly remembered keeping it open.

I told myself a draft could have pushed it closed, but I knew none of the windows were open, since I liked to be kept in the quiet when I worked.

I stood out of my chair, still feeling unnerved, and went over to open the door again. The moment my fingers touched the handle, I felt a strong presence behind me, the temperature in the room dropping very suddenly.

I froze, my heart lurching in my chest.

I was too scared to turn around. My body was reacting to *something*, and I was too frightened to see what it was.

I felt a breeze on my neck, even though the windows were closed, strong enough to stir some strands of hair across my skin.

It really felt like someone was stood directly behind me, breathing on my neck. Every nerve in my body was convinced as much.

I turned slowly, not sure what I was expecting. Nothing.

There was nothing there.

I let out a slow, shaky breath. And for just a moment, I thought I heard, mingling with my own, another, more ragged sound, like a whisper, or a gasp, that did not belong to me.

Then the room grew lighter, warmer, and whatever had been there with me finally left.

I tried to forget the incident, and didn't tell my husband when he came home later that day. I chalked it down to being tired, or overworked, or stressed about my grandma's passing. Anything but the idea of something paranormal. Because I knew that was nothing but sensational stories designed to scare and trick people.

I was reluctant for my husband to leave the next morning. I no longer wanted to be in the house alone, even though I figured it was all in my mind.

Once he left, I went round making sure all the windows and doors were locked. Just in case. Just for an extra sense of security, and peace of mind.

I headed to my office to start working, even pausing to put something in front of the door to prevent it from closing again.

It was a dreary morning; rain pattered against the windows, casting a dull veneer over everything, so I switched on the desk lamp to try alleviate some of the shadows creeping around the room.

Even just the simple orange glow of the light reassured me somewhat, and I sat down to begin working, resting my fingers on the keyboard.

An hour passed, undisturbed. I was just starting to slip into a working haze when the light flickered off, plunging me into sudden gloom.

I gave a start, my gaze flicking from the computer screen to the lamp.

Had the bulb blown?

The light flickered back on and off again with a low buzz, creating a strange undulation of light and shadow around the room.

It was definitely faulty. I shouldn't risk leaving it switched on.

Just as I was about to reach for the lamp switch, the chair I was sitting on jolted backwards across the carpet, and I elicited a soft, muffled scream.

What the hell?

My pulse skyrocketed as I glanced down, trying to figure out what had pushed me. The chair was on wheels, but it still needed a good force to be yanked backwards like that.

Scared it would happen again, I stood up and backed away from the desk.

What was *happening*?

Like before, the temperature in the room dropped suddenly, and all the hairs on my arms stood up. There was something here. Something I couldn't see. Something I couldn't explain.

The desk lamp began to flicker again, the buzzing getting louder. I thought it was going to explode.

Without waiting to see what was going to happen, I ran out of the room, leaving the door open behind me.

Whatever it was didn't follow me. I headed downstairs, my heart racing in my chest, my head spinning.

My hands trembled as I turned on the kitchen tap and filled a glass of water. I could barely swallow it, my mouth was so dry.

As much as I didn't want to, I had to accept that something strange was going on. Something *paranormal.* That's what they called things you couldn't see, right? Phenomena that was impossible to explain. Beyond the scope of human understanding.

I was being haunted. By what, I had no idea.

As I sipped slowly on the water, I heard something thud against the ceiling above me, making my heart lurch.

Had something fallen?

Another thud, and then another, all hitting the floor with soft vibrations.

It was coming from my office, directly overhead.

Although I was terrified to go up there, I set down the glass of water and grabbed a knife from the drawer. I don't know what it would do against something I couldn't see, but I felt safer with it.

Slowly, I crept back upstairs. The thudding had stopped now, but somehow, that didn't reassure me. I got the sense that whatever it was, it was waiting. It had got my attention, and now it was waiting for me to step inside the room.

Heart thudding dully in my ears, I peered around the doorway, into the office.

The floor was a mess. Books and pens and folders were scattered across the carpet. They had all been knocked off the shelf.

The only thing that remained standing, amid the chaos, was the vase. The vase I had inherited from my grandma.

My heart sunk. My throat went dry again.

Then it all made sense. None of this had started happening until I brought that vase into my home.

Was *that* the reason I was being plagued by this entity? Was the *vase* the thing that was haunted, not me?

As soon as I made that connection, I marched over to the vase and grasped it between my hands, dropping the knife. For a moment, I felt another breath on the back of my neck, an ice-cold touch, but I ignored it, marching out of the room with the vase in tow.

I didn't want to destroy it, since it was a gift from my grandma, but if I temporarily re-located it, then maybe the activity would stop in my house.

I decided to box it back up in the dozens of layers of bubble wrap, and store it in the shed outside.

That way, whatever energy was attached to the vase, would be trapped somewhere it couldn't hurt me or my husband.

REAL GHOST STORY

Shudder

I borrowed the camera from my teacher, Mrs. Thompson, without any inkling of the horrors that would unfold. It was a beautiful vintage piece, with its worn leather casing and intricate brass details. Mrs. Thompson, always encouraging my passion for photography, entrusted me with it, hoping I would capture moments of beauty and wonder.

Little did I know that the weekend I took the camera would be forever etched in my memory as a time of darkness and despair. A hurricane ravaged our small town, its fierce winds and torrential rain tearing through the streets, leaving destruction in its wake. The storm was merciless, and amidst the chaos, tragedy struck.

Mrs. Thompson, with her kind heart and adventurous spirit, had ventured out into the tempestuous night, perhaps to help others in need or to brave the elements for some unknown reason. She never returned. News of her demise during the hurricane spread quickly, casting a shadow over the entire community. I was devastated by the loss of my teacher, mentor, and friend.

In the days that followed, I resolved to return the camera to Mrs. Thompson's grieving family. It seemed only right to honor her memory by giving back what she had entrusted to me. With a heavy heart, I made my way to her home, a quaint cottage nestled on the outskirts of town.

As I stood on the doorstep, a sense of foreboding washed over me, as if the very air carried whispers of an unseen presence. Mrs. Thompson's family welcomed me warmly, their eyes filled with sorrow. They insisted I keep the camera, explaining that it was the last thing she had given me, and that it held a special significance. I tried to protest, but they were resolute. Reluctantly, I accepted their offer, knowing that this camera would forever be a reminder of the teacher I had lost.

One evening, as I sat alone in the dimly lit room, the air heavy with the scent of developer chemicals, I carefully studied the photographs that had just emerged from the darkroom. They were my latest works, capturing the essence of the abandoned mansion on the outskirts of town. The flickering light of the candles, the peeling wallpaper, and the decaying furniture all held a certain allure that drew me in. But as I gazed at the developed prints, a chill ran down my spine, as though an icy finger traced its way along my vertebrae.

Dark, shadowy figures lurked in the background of the photographs, their forms distorted and indistinct, like phantoms emerging from the depths of my subconscious. They seemed to melt into the surroundings, blending seamlessly with the crumbling walls and the inky blackness of the corners. Their presence, barely visible, sent a shiver through my soul, as if they possessed some malevolent purpose that defied explanation.

I had not noticed them while capturing the shots, my focus consumed by the grandeur of the mansion's ruinous beauty. But now they revealed themselves, hauntingly etched into the images, like secrets whispered by unseen lips. Their enigmatic nature fueled my curiosity, yet a sense of unease gnawed at my core.

Unable to contain my growing apprehension, I decided to share the photographs with my friends, hoping their rational minds could provide an explanation that eluded me. Gathering them in my parlor, we sat around the mahogany table, the photographs laid out before us like evidence in a macabre trial.

Silence enveloped the room as their eyes scanned the images, and I watched their expressions morph into mirrors of my own unease. The atmosphere grew thick with trepidation, as if the room itself had become a receptacle for our collective fear. Whispers of disbelief and uncertainty filled the air, mingling with the faint scent of old books and the distant echoes of a clock's ticking.

"What are these figures?" my friend Amelia finally ventured, her voice trembling slightly. "They seem otherworldly, as if they exist beyond the realm of our understanding."

I nodded, my heart pounding in my chest. "I've never encountered anything like this before," I confessed, my voice barely above a whisper. "The camera captured something... something that defies explanation, something that lies hidden from our mortal sight."

The others nodded, their faces pale, their eyes reflecting a mixture of fascination and fear. We delved into a heated discussion, each of us offering theories that danced on the border between reality and superstition. Were they ghosts, lingering spirits trapped within the mansion's decaying walls? Or perhaps they were demons, summoned by some dark ritual that had long been forgotten. The possibilities seemed endless, and yet, each explanation felt insufficient, unable to capture the true essence of the enigmatic figures.

One night, as I sat on the worn-out couch, seeking solace from the relentless haunting of the photographs that lined the walls, a heavy silence settled upon the house. The dim light from the flickering candle barely illuminated the room, casting eerie shadows that danced across the peeling wallpaper. The air was thick with anticipation, as if something ominous lurked just beyond the veil of my perception.

As I trembled on the couch, the fabric rough against my clammy skin, a cold draft enveloped the room, seeping into my very bones. I huddled closer to myself, desperately seeking warmth that eluded me. It was then that I felt it—a touch, a graze against my skin, as if an invisible hand had reached out to reassure me or, perhaps, to claim me as its own.

The sensation was both gentle and unnerving, like icy tendrils brushing against my flesh. I shivered involuntarily, goosebumps rising in response to this ethereal caress. It was as though I had become a vessel, a conduit for the paranormal forces that swirled around me. They tugged and pulled at my very being, their unseen fingers tracing a path along my spine, leaving me breathless and terrified.

Every photograph I take now carries a weight of uncertainty, a fear of what may manifest within its depths. The world around me has become a realm of perpetual unease, where the line between the living and the spectral blurs. The camera, once a tool of artistic expression, has transformed into a conduit for the supernatural.

Sleep eludes me as nightmares haunt my nights, visions of those ethereal figures lurking in the shadows, waiting to claim me. Their presence lingers in the corners of my vision, a constant reminder that I am forever touched by the otherworldly.

I have tried to seek solace in rational explanations, to convince myself that it is all a figment of my imagination. But the undeniable truth remains, etched into my memories and captured within those haunted photographs. The camera holds a power beyond comprehension, a window into a world unseen.

I have contemplated destroying it, erasing this source of terror from my life. But a part of me hesitates, unsure of the consequences that may follow. What if the camera's malevolence extends beyond its physical form? What if destroying it only intensifies the haunting, unleashing a torrent of vengeful spirits?

So, I keep it, hidden away in a corner of my room, a constant reminder of the darkness that envelops me. It serves as a reminder of the fragility of our existence, the thin veil that separates the tangible from the intangible.

In the end, I am left to navigate this haunting existence, forever changed by the events that unfolded. The camera, once a symbol of artistic passion and connection, now stands as a testament to the eerie and inexplicable. I am but a witness to the unknown, forever marked by the camera's chilling gaze.

REAL GHOST STORY

Shadow Rider

I stood at the threshold of my twin daughters' bedroom, a gentle smile on my lips as I watched them snuggle beneath their cozy blankets. It had been a few weeks since we moved into our new home, an old Victorian house with a charm that whispered stories of decades past. It was a house that seemed to hold secrets, secrets that were slowly revealing themselves.

As I prepared to bid my girls goodnight, my gaze fell upon the vintage rocking horse we had discovered in the attic, left behind by the previous owners. Its aged wooden frame, adorned with intricate carvings, had caught my attention the moment I set eyes on it. It seemed like the perfect addition to my daughters' room, a whimsical toy that would transport them to a world of imagination.

With a gentle tug, I pulled the bedroom door closed, enveloping the room in a warm, comforting darkness. But just as I turned away, a soft creaking sound reached my ears, causing a shiver to run down my spine. I turned back, my gaze drawn to the rocking horse.

To my astonishment, the rocking horse moved on its own, rocking back and forth without any visible cause. I rubbed my eyes, convinced that it was a trick of the light or a figment of my tired imagination. But no matter how hard I blinked; the rocking horse continued its eerie dance.

Fear gnawed at the edges of my mind. Could there be something more to this antique toy? Could there be a presence lingering within its wooden frame, something unseen that defied explanation? A chill settled over me as I hurriedly left the room, vowing to keep a watchful eye on the mysterious rocking horse.

Days turned into weeks, and life settled into a comforting rhythm within the old house. My daughters, oblivious to the strange occurrence with the rocking horse, reveled in their innocent laughter and the joy the house brought them. But deep down, I couldn't shake the feeling that something was amiss.

One evening, as twilight bathed the house in a cascade of fading sunlight, my daughters burst into my room, their faces etched with fear. Their tiny hands clung to mine, their voices trembling as they described what they had witnessed.

"Mommy, there was a dark shadow figure sitting on the rocking horse," they whispered in unison, their eyes wide with terror. "It was rocking back and forth, back and forth, but we couldn't see its face."

My heart skipped a beat as their words echoed in my ears. The presence I had suspected had revealed itself to my daughters, its eerie silhouette haunting their innocent dreams. I hugged them tightly, feeling the weight of responsibility settle upon my shoulders.

Together, we ventured back into their bedroom, the flickering glow of a nightlight casting long shadows upon the walls. As we reached the rocking horse, a shiver ran through the air, an inexplicable coldness that left our skin tingling. I held my breath, my eyes darting around the room, searching for any sign of the dark figure my daughters had described.

But the room remained still, silent, as though it held its

breath alongside us. The rocking horse stood motionless, its carved features frozen in time. I couldn't deny the unease that settled deep within me, but I knew I had to protect my children.

With a heavy heart, I made the decision to part ways with the antique rocking horse. Its presence had become a source of unease and fear, and I couldn't bear to see my daughters frightened any longer. I knew it was time to sever the connection between the mysterious rocking horse and our lives.

I carefully lifted the rocking horse, its weight heavier than I remembered, and carried it down to the basement. There, amongst the forgotten relics and dusty corners, I found a cardboard box, a vessel for the secrets we wished to bury. I placed the rocking horse inside, its carved features gazing up at me one last time, as if bidding farewell.

As I closed the lid, a wave of relief washed over me. It was an act of letting go, of releasing the hold that the rocking horse had over our lives. I knew that the memories of its haunting presence would linger, forever etched in our minds, but it was a chapter we had to close.

It wasn't long before the house regained its sense of peace. My daughters' laughter filled the air once more, their innocence restored. We moved forward, embracing the warmth and joy that our new home had to offer.

Yet, deep within, I knew that I would never forget the rocking horse and the creepy ordeal that surrounded it. It served as a reminder that there are mysteries in this world that defy explanation, that sometimes we must confront the unknown and make choices to protect those we love.

REAL GHOST STORY

Bargain Hunters

One of my family's favorite things to do is go around to the thrift stores throughout the areas we live in and see what kinds of treasures we can find. My mother and I used to do this and the bargain-hunting bug seems to have been passed on to my own children. Something happened a few years ago however that left me questioning the safety of bringing strange objects into our home.

My son Michael had just turned 10, still young enough to like some of the toys that were inevitably discarded by other children as they grew up. Still, he was getting old enough that it had to be something a little more grown-up than a stuffed animal. One day we were looking through the shelves and he came up to me with what looked like an old metal toy car. He was over the moon with his find and I knew that if I didn't agree to get it for him it was going to break his heart. The store only wanted a few dollars for it so I told him he could get it.

Like many toys that had come before Michael played with the car for a little over a week before it seemed to vanish into thin air, replaced by the next great find from the secondhand store. That is why I was surprised to find it sitting in the middle of the floor a couple of months later, seemingly abandoned there by my son.

I told him he shouldn't leave his toys out in the middle of the floor because it could be dangerous. Like many kids his age when confronted about this he claimed that he didn't put it there. Michael however is an only child and I know I wouldn't have left the car there so I just assumed he didn't want to put his toy away, a regular occurrence in our household. After a short disagreement, he huffed off and begrudgingly put the car back in his closet.

Finding the car in random places started to become a regular thing. Every time Michael would claim to be innocent of the offense but there was really no explanation for it being out other than him. Finally, I reached the end of my patience with him when I found it right outside my door. By finding it on this particular occasion I mean I stepped on it and hurled a number of curses at the toy. To teach him a lesson I hid the toy at the top of my closet thinking that he would just have to go without it for a while.

To my surprise he didn't ask about its whereabouts once. Then, about a week later I found the toy sitting on the floor of the kitchen. I was beside myself with anger thinking my son had gone through my room looking for the toy without my permission. When he told me that it wasn't him I grounded him for lying to me. I just didn't know what else to do other than find a better hiding spot for the toy. That place ended up being the attic in our house since I figured there would be no way he would find it there.

That same night I woke up to the sound of something moving coming from the ceiling. I don't know why but the first thought that came into my head was somehow Michael had snuck up there and was playing with that damn car. I didn't even bother looking in his room as I walked by and pulled the cord to release the latch to the attic.

When I climbed up I could already tell something was off since the area was pitch black and the ladder had still been up in the ceiling. The lights back in the hallway provided enough light for me to find the pull string attached to the light and with a loud click the space came into view.

Our attic, like most other people's, was full of boxes that contained a lifetime's worth of possessions one is not willing to part with yet we were unwilling to put on display. Everything was covered in a fine layer of dust with the exception of my son's toy car which sat alone in the middle of the floor. The other thing I saw was the footprints that riddled the surface as if someone had been running around but the size of them was far too small to be that of my son's.

My first thought was that some child had made his/her way into our home and had somehow kept us from seeing them but that seemed farfetched even with the evidence right out in the open like this, but what other explanation could there be? Almost like it was trying to answer my question the car, seemingly on its own moved forward a couple of inches towards me. I took an involuntary step backward and would have probably taken more had it not been for the hole that I'd climbed up sitting right behind me.

I sat there, staring at the toy, not sure if I'd really just seen it move on its own when it happened again, this time through the toy covered half the distance between me and it. That was enough to send me scrambling as fast as I could back down the ladder and shoving it back up into the ceiling, sealing the car and whatever was causing it to move up there.

I made my way back into the living room and sat down on the couch, trying to collect my thoughts. How could a toy move on its own? It was the thing that was bouncing around inside my head. It was possible the ceiling wasn't level and the car was simply rolling down a slight incline but how did the toy get there in the first place, not to mention the footprints that marred the floor.

I'd always considered myself someone who was open to the possibility of the supernatural but to have it smack me in the face like this, I was totally unprepared. The following day I asked my husband to go up to the attic and get the car so we could get rid of it. When he went up there though there was no sign of the toy, even after I asked him to look around to see if he could find it there was no trace of it anywhere.

That was the last night I ever heard any sounds coming from the attic and the car stopped showing up in random spots around the house. For both of those things I was thankful, but I still wonder what actually happened to the car and if was there some sort of spirit of a child that was attached to it that I brought into my home when we bought it. Maybe those are two questions that are better left unanswered in the end.

REAL GHOST STORY

Strings Attached...

REAL GHOST STORY

Strings Attached...

As I huddled there, shaking, under the covers of my bed I couldn't help but wonder if I was to blame for what was happening right now. It was, after all, my decision to purchase the odd-looking marionette online in the first place. It was I who clicked the Buy Now button on that online auction site. I didn't know that I was also going to receive something else as well.

Don't misunderstand me when I tell you there was something attached to the marionette. He didn't get up and walk and he didn't move from place to place with no explanation. He wasn't one of those kind of haunted objects. Gary, as I had named him, carried with him a spirit that traveled wherever he went, a paranormal hitchhiker if you will. Had I known I was getting a two-for-one special with my purchase I probably would have thought twice about adding him to my ever-growing collection.

As I just told you, I collect marionettes and have for a number of years. A lot of people would incorrectly call them "puppets," but they'd be wrong. The primary difference between the two is that a marionette is controlled by a series of strings attached to a mechanism that is held by a person whereas a puppet is not. It's a common mistake, but for those who collect like I do, a difference we find ourselves explaining far too often.

Despite what I know now, you could say that I was smitten with Gary from the moment that I saw his picture online. He was an antique clown with a black and white outfit and a white cone hat. His face was painted to match his outfit with black encircling his eyes. The only bit of color on him was the small red smile he had. Sure, he checked a few boxes that would have made most people label him as creepy, but I thought he was amazing. Plus, I could make him mine for only twenty bucks. It felt like a no-brainer.

It took just over a week before the box containing Gary arrived on my front porch. To say I tore it open just like I had done to the presents I received as a child would be an understatement. As soon as I had him in my hands I just knew I'd made the right choice in buying him. I had even cleared off a place on a shelf in my guest room where much of the marionettes I'd collected were kept to put him.

For nearly two weeks, nothing happened, or at least I didn't notice anything odd going on in my house. Then I found myself waking up at odd hours for six straight nights. When this would happen I found myself instantly awake and my adrenaline up. My body was at the height of its fight or flight reaction but the reason for it was lost on me. I would sit there, in my bed, listening for anything out of place and for the first week of this nothing stood out to me.

On the seventh night, I clearly heard a knocking sound coming from an area next to my bed. It wasn't just one single knock, but a series of two or three sharp raps. This particular wall was one that separated the master bedroom and the guest room. I was sure someone had broken into my home and I had to decide what I was going to do. I had two choices, either grab the bat that I kept next to my door in case someone tried to venture into my bedroom or hide and hope for the best.

In the end I didn't do either of these things. Instead, I grabbed the bat and go on the offensive. After opening the door as quietly as I could and made the fifteen-foot walk down the hall. Before I could change my mind I reached out and grabbed the handle and flung the door open with a scream hoping to startle whomever had infiltrated my house.

To my surprise, the room was empty. I checked the lock on the sill and found it engaged. For someone to break in and lock the window seemed odd but I can't say that I'm an expert on breaking and entering. I kept the bat at the ready and checked the closet and behind the door to no effect. From there I moved further out, making sure every place where I thought someone could hide and checking every lock. Despite finding no one and every lock engaged I couldn't settle myself enough to get back to sleep for the rest of the night.

Finding myself awake between 1:00-3:00 am had already become a nightly occurrence but when the knocking was added to it I no longer felt safe inside my home. I'd heard stories of people hiding in basements or attics for extended periods of time only to come out and slay the unsuspecting homeowners at night while they slept. I even went so far as to call the police and have them check the home for signs of intruders to no avail.

The idea of a ghost being in my home didn't even occur to me until one evening when I was sitting up in bed reading a book and all of a sudden I felt the mattress sink a little to one side, almost as if someone had sat down on the edge. I don't have any pets and I live alone so the sudden change was alarming. Even when I looked up I could see the place on the bed where for all I could tell someone was sitting yet I couldn't see anyone there.

It was then that every hair on my body seemed to stand on end and the room seemed to drop in temperature. I'm not sure if this was my body's reaction to the unexplainable or if it was whatever or whoever it was sitting at the end of my bed causing a shift in the atmosphere but every part of my brain was yelling to me that I wasn't alone in my room even if I couldn't see anyone there.

Now that I'd recognized its presence in my home the spirit seemed to get bolder. Numerous times I felt like someone was watching me and on a few occasions I felt like someone ran their fingers through my hair or tapped me on the shoulder. Even though the things the ghost was doing weren't outright violent, the intrusion was very unsettling. The thing I didn't understand at the time though was how this had happened. What had changed in order to introduce something like this into my home? I racked my brain, trying to think of what had changed recently, and then something in the back of my mind clicked.

Gary. He was the most recent addition to my home. As I went back through the timeline of events it made more and more sense. Everything that was going on started shortly after he arrived. To me the answer was simple, if I got rid of the marionette then all of my problems should resolve themselves.

The following day I took Gary and the box he had come in to the local thrift shop, convinced my problems were over. Despite how much I liked him I was not willing to put up with a supernatural squatter in order to keep him. When I returned home I already felt lighter and was looking forward to having the first uninterrupted night of sleep I'd had in almost a month.

And now we have come full circle. Here I am, huddled under the covers as the light knocking has moved from the guest bedroom to my own. Despite getting rid of Gary it seems the spirit has now taken up residence in my home. Is it now my home that this ghost is attached to or worse yet, is it me? I made the mistake of bringing something into my house, inviting in with it an energy that seems quite content to stay right where it's at.

I don't know how much longer I can take this. It is affecting both my personal and professional life and there's no end in sight. If I move and the ghost follows me, then what am I supposed to do? I just don't know.

REAL GHOST STORY

Nightmare Box

It all started on a dreary Saturday morning when my father and I ventured out to our beloved weekend ritual—a yard sale extravaganza. The air was thick with anticipation as we perused the rows of discarded treasures, hoping to stumble upon a hidden gem. Amidst the jumble of forgotten trinkets and dusty relics, I discovered a weathered Jack-in-the-box toy.

Its once vibrant colors had faded, and the wooden box bore the scars of time, but there was something oddly compelling about it. Intrigued, I handed over a few coins to the elderly vendor, who offered a cryptic smile as the transaction was completed.

Little did I know that this innocent acquisition would mark the beginning of a sinister chapter in my life. As the sun dipped below the horizon and darkness cloaked the world, I brought the Jack-in-the-box home, my fingers tracing the intricate carvings on its surface.

That night, as I lay in bed, a faint sound pierced the silence—a haunting melody, faint yet unmistakable. The tune emanated from the Jack-in-the-box, its eerie chimes echoing through the empty corridors of my home. My heart raced, and my breath caught in my throat as the melody grew louder, more insistent. I could sense a malevolent presence lurking within the room, its unseen eyes fixed upon me.

Terrified, I mustered the courage to investigate, clutching a flashlight in my trembling hand. The pale beam of light exposed the darkness, revealing nothing but the lifeless walls and the Jack-in-the-box perched on a dusty shelf. Perspiration trickled down my brow as I reached out to touch the toy, but as my hand drew near, the haunting melody abruptly ceased, leaving me shrouded in an eerie silence.

Days turned into weeks, and the once-harmless toy continued to torment me. Each night, like a harbinger of dread, it would spring to life, its lid creaking open with a spine-chilling screech. The painted visage of a grinning clown would leer at me, its eyes filled with a malevolence that seemed to seep into my very soul.

I pleaded with my parents, desperate for them to understand the terror that had invaded our home. But they scoffed at my fears, dismissing them as mere imaginings of an overactive mind. They could not hear the whispers that echoed in the dead of night, nor witness the chilling dance of shadows cast by that cursed toy.

Then, one fateful night, as the moon hung low in the sky, I awoke to an unfamiliar sound—a faint clicking noise. My heart pounded in my chest as I strained my ears, following the source of the noise. It seemed to originate from the corner of my room where the Jack-in-the-box lay, its lid tightly shut.

With trepidation gripping my every nerve, I reached out to switch on the light, illuminating the room in a soft glow. But the sight that greeted me was far from reassuring. The Jack-in-the-box sat innocently on the shelf, yet I could swear I heard the sound of someone winding it up—an invisible hand turning the rusty crank with a purpose.

A cold shiver slithered down my spine, and a sense of

impending doom settled upon me like a suffocating fog. Fear consumed me as I frantically searched the room, my eyes darting from corner to corner, half-expecting a malevolent presence to materialize before me. But there was nothing. No one.

The clicking sound persisted, growing louder and more pronounced with each passing second. I was certain that I was not alone in that room, that unseen eyes watched my every move. Drawing a deep breath, I summoned the courage to approach the Jack-in-the-box, its lid now trembling with an ominous energy.

As my hand trembled, I hesitated for a moment, the weight of the unknown bearing down upon me. With a trembling grip, I turned the crank, the gears grinding with a macabre symphony. The tension in the air thickened, suffocating me as I waited for what horrors would unfold.

With a sudden release, the lid sprang open, and a jester's face burst forth, its grotesque grin stretching impossibly wide. The clown's eyes, once innocent and playful, now glinted with a malevolence that chilled me to the bone. Its laughter, a haunting melody, filled the room, drowning out my own cries of terror.

I stumbled backward, my heart pounding against my ribcage as I tried to escape the clutches of that cursed toy. But no matter how far I ran, its laughter followed, echoing through the corridors of my mind. It became a torment, a constant reminder of the darkness that had descended upon my life.

Weeks turned into months, and my nights were plagued by relentless nightmares—visions of sinister clowns dancing in a hall of mirrors, their distorted reflections mocking my every fear. Sleep became a battleground, and I dared not close my eyes for fear of what lurked in the shadows of my dreams.

Finally, unable to bear the torment any longer, I made a decision. I would rid myself of the cursed Jack-in-the-box once and for all. With trembling hands, I carefully wrapped it in layers of newspaper, shielding the malevolence it held within. The weight of the darkness seemed to seep into my very bones as I tossed it into the trash, its lid forever sealed.

As the garbage truck rumbled away, carrying with it the embodiment of my nightmares, a sense of relief washed over me. The house, once suffocated by a palpable darkness, seemed to breathe again. Sunlight streamed through the windows, casting away the shadows that had haunted me for far too long.

But deep within, a lingering unease remained—a scar etched upon my soul. I had glimpsed into the abyss, and though I had escaped its clutches, I knew that the horrors I had faced would forever remain a part of me. The Jack-in-the-box may have been gone, but its malevolent presence lingered in the recesses of my mind, a constant reminder of the fragility of innocence and the darkness that can lurk within the most innocuous of objects.

And so, I walked forward, forever changed by that harrowing encounter. The nightmares may have subsided, but a part of me knew that the shadows would always be there, waiting, just beyond the edge of perception, ready to remind me that evil can wear the face of a clown.

REAL GHOST STORY

Enchanted Illusions

I stumbled upon a peculiar magic set at a flea market. I was just eleven years old, but the allure of illusions and wonderment was too enticing to resist. With my heart racing, I handed over my hard-earned allowance and clutched the box tightly, eager to unlock the secrets within.

Arriving home, I couldn't contain my excitement. I hurriedly tore open the packaging, revealing an array of mysterious objects—sleight of hand tricks, decks of cards, and a worn top hat that seemed to hold endless possibilities. My mind whirled with visions of grand performances, of dazzling my family with my newfound abilities.

That evening, I transformed my bedroom into a makeshift stage. I adorned myself in a makeshift magician's cape, hastily fashioned from an old bedsheet, and placed my hat upon my head with a flourish. With trembling hands, I practiced each trick meticulously, determined to perfect the art of deception.

As the night wore on, a peculiar sound disrupted the stillness of my room—an eerie scratching, like skeletal fingers tracing the surface of my headboard. Ignoring the disconcerting noise, I pressed on, determined to captivate my audience. It was only when I retired to my bed, fatigue tugging at my eyelids, that the true nature of the scratching began to unnerve me.

In the depths of darkness, as whispers of dreams began to dance through my mind, the scratching grew louder, more insistent. It seemed to echo from within the walls, as though a phantom creature sought to claw its way into my sanctuary. Fear lodged itself in my throat, and I pulled the covers over my head, praying for morning's arrival.

The following night, I awoke to a chilling realization.

My beloved magic set, carefully returned to its box the previous evening, had mysteriously vanished. Panic coursed through my veins as I frantically searched every corner of the house. Yet, no matter how diligently I scoured each room, the elusive box remained hidden from my grasp.

Confusion and trepidation wrapped around my heart like a vise. How could my cherished possessions vanish without a trace? The unease settled deep within me, casting a shadow over my once joyful spirit. Each night, the eerie occurrences escalated, like a dark symphony gaining momentum.

It was the third night when I awoke, bleary-eyed and disoriented, to answer nature's call. The house was shrouded in a cloak of midnight, the only illumination emanating from the pale glow of the moon. As I stumbled towards the bathroom, I noticed peculiar shapes dancing upon the walls—a grotesque masquerade of sinister silhouettes.

My breath caught in my throat, frozen in the grip of terror. The shadows twisted and contorted, assuming the forms of faceless figures, their elongated limbs stretching and contracting like ethereal marionettes. I rubbed my eyes, willing the macabre vision to dissipate, but the haunting specters remained, leering at me from the confines of the darkness.

Fear propelled me forward, and with trembling hands, I flicked on the bathroom light, banishing the unholy apparitions. My heart pounded within my chest, a cacophony of dread. I couldn't bear to spend another moment in that house, plagued by the inexplicable and sinister.

In a desperate bid to rid myself of the malevolence that had invaded my sanctuary, I made a decision that would forever alter my path. The following day, I gathered my disheveled magician's cape, my trembling hands clutching the remnants of my once-beloved magic set. Determined to sever the ties that bound me to this inexplicable terror, I set out to donate my cherished possessions to the local youth ranch.

The sun hung high in the sky, casting a golden glow upon the vibrant autumn leaves as I approached the youth ranch. The worn wooden sign creaked in the gentle breeze, welcoming me to a place of hope and new beginnings. As I stepped through the entrance, my heart swelled with a mixture of apprehension and relief.

A group of children played in the courtyard, their laughter echoing through the air like a balm to my troubled soul. The weight of the supernatural burden I had carried for days began to lift, replaced by a glimmer of optimism. Perhaps, in sharing the magic set with these deserving young souls, I could find solace and break free from the clutches of the unknown.

I entered the main building, my footsteps resonating against the creaking floorboards. The walls were adorned with vibrant drawings, each stroke a testament to the resilience and creativity of these children. The air carried a sense of innocence and purity, a stark contrast to the shadows that had plagued my nights.

Approaching the reception desk, I was greeted by a warm smile. A woman with kind eyes and a gentle demeanor welcomed me, her voice filled with compassion. "How can we assist you today?" she asked, her genuine interest evident.

Summoning the remnants of my courage, I explained my strange encounter, the vanishing magic set, and the nightmarish shadows that had haunted my dreams. The woman listened intently, her brows furrowing with empathy. "It sounds like you've been through quite an ordeal," she said softly. "But I believe your donation will bring joy to these children, and perhaps, in giving away the source of your fear, you'll find peace."

Her words resonated within me, and with a renewed sense of purpose, I handed over the magic set. The woman's eyes sparkled as she examined each item, her fingers tracing the worn edges and faded colors. "Thank you," she whispered, her voice filled with gratitude. "I'm sure the children will cherish these gifts."

As I turned to leave, a weight lifted from my shoulders, replaced by a newfound lightness of being. The strange occurrences that had plagued my nights seemed to fade into the background, swallowed by the warmth and hope that enveloped the youth ranch. The echoes of scratching and the haunting shadows retreated, leaving me in a state of tranquility I had not known for weeks.

Months passed, and the memory of those eerie nights began to fade, like a distant dream. The magic set remained in the safekeeping of the youth ranch, sparking joy and imagination in the hearts of those who needed it most. As for me, I embarked on a journey of self-discovery, exploring new passions and pursuits that allowed me to leave the shadows of the past behind.

Sometimes, in the stillness of the night, I would lay in bed, recalling the chilling whispers and the dance of the spectral shadows. Yet, they held no power over me anymore. The magic set, once a source of fascination turned nightmare, had transformed into a catalyst for growth and resilience.

REAL GHOST STORY

Swaying Spirits

As a child, I was drawn to the outdoors like a moth to a flame. Nature held a magnetic pull over me - its mysteries and wonders beckoning at every turn. Whether given the choice between sitting indoors in front of a flickering screen or venturing outside to explore the untamed world, I always chose the latter. The call of adventure, the invigorating sensation of fresh air on my skin, and the thrill of running through fields or climbing trees consumed my every thought.

But then it happened. When I was just eight years old,

my family abruptly moved to a new house in a quiet little neighborhood. My father's job had led us here, and while I understood the reasons for our relocation, I couldn't help but feel a pang of sadness. The house, though equipped with a sizable yard, seemed devoid of anything that would fuel my outdoor escapades.

Days turned into weeks, and as time passed, my disappointment grew. Until one fateful day, my father came hurrying into the house brimming with excitement. He had found something truly special, something he knew would bring joy to my young heart - a swing set. It had been the unexpected outcome of an estate sale down the street, left behind by a neighbor who had suddenly passed away.

The moment we brought that swing set into our backyard, I felt an eeriness settle over it. The air held a tangibility, a whisper of the supernatural. The first ghostly incident occurred when I took a seat on one of the swings. No sooner had I begun to swing back and forth, a force unseen pushed me, causing me to soar higher and faster than I had intended. Panic welled up within me as I struggled to regain control, my heart pounding in my chest. What unseen presence had taken hold?

Another spine-chilling occurrence transpired during the icy grip of winter. I trudged through the snow, bundled up in layers of clothing, towards the swing set. As I approached, the chains of the swings rattled and swung violently, as if being played with by an invisible entity. My breath caught in my throat, and a shiver crept down my spine. I couldn't comprehend what I was witnessing - the inexplicable movement of the swings defied all logic.

But it was the final encounter that forever etched itself into my memory. It was a quiet morning, and I found myself sitting in the cozy warmth of our kitchen, transfixed by the serene beauty of the falling snow outside. I gazed through the frosted windowpane, captivated by the delicate dance of the snowflakes. Yet, as my eyes scanned past the windowpane to the swing set, I was met with a sight that chilled me to the core.

A group of spectral figures, almost translucent, sat upon the swings. They swayed back and forth in an unhurried rhythm, their movements ethereal and soundless. These ghostly apparitions appeared to be children, their features distorted and hazy, as if time had long since forgotten their existence. Their presence sent a surge of icy unease flooding my veins, and I quickly averted my gaze, unable to tear my eyes away from the haunting scene.

From that day forward, I vowed to never venture near

that swing set again. Its inexplicable happenings, the unsettling encounters with the supernatural, had left an indelible mark on my childhood memories. Though I couldn't definitively say the swing set was haunted, the inexplicable occurrences that transpired there were enough to keep me away.

And so, as time passed and I grew into adulthood, the swing set in our backyard became a relic of my youth. Its rusted chains and faded seats stood as a silent testament to the mysteries that had unfolded in my childhood home. The memories, both captivating and bone-chilling, still lingered in my mind, a constant reminder that even the most ordinary objects could hold secrets, hidden in the shadows of the unknown.

REAL GHOST STORY

Ghost Express

REAL GHOST
STORY

Ghost Express

For Christmas, when I was 6, my grandpa got me an antique train set. That was my last holiday with my grandfather before he passed away, so I cherished the gift. I loved it. At first. After a few months, things started to take a strange turn.

The train set, once a source of joy and wonder, became the catalyst for an eerie series of events that would haunt my young mind for years to come. One night, in the dead silence of darkness, I would hear faint whispers emanating from the corner of my room where the train set stood proudly. The whispers, barely audible, grew louder and more perplexing as the nights passed.

Nervous and sleep-deprived, I would roll over, desperately trying to shake off the unnerving feeling that something sinister was lurking within the shadows. But no matter how much I tried to ignore it, the whispers persisted like a macabre lullaby, echoing through the walls of my bedroom.

Weeks turned into a month, and the unsettling occurrences intensified. One fateful night, my dreams were shattered by an inexplicable event. The train set, which had remained dormant until then, abruptly sprung to life. Its wheels screeched against the rails, filling the room with a cacophony of sound that pierced through the silence.

As I sat up in bed, my heart pounding in my chest, I watched in both awe and terror as the miniature locomotive chugged along the tracks, seemingly guided by an unseen force. The train's haunting whistle echoed within the room, sending chills down my spine. But this was not the end of the bizarre spectacle.

As if in defiance of the natural order, the train suddenly derailed, its wheels grinding to a halt. The room fell into a profound silence, broken only by the echo of my rapid breaths. Trembling, I mustered the courage to approach the fallen train, its twisted metal and shattered cargo a stark reminder of the darkness that lurked beneath the surface.

Days turned into weeks, and the air was thick with a growing sense of foreboding. It was during one of my solitary play sessions with the train set that the room itself seemed to come alive with a malevolent energy. The lights flickered with an unnerving rhythm, casting ominous shadows on the wall behind the train.

I watched in fearful fascination as one particular shadow, distorted and elongated, began to take the form of a man. The figure seemed ethereal, its twisted silhouette dancing against the wall as if controlled by some unseen puppeteer. Even when I summoned the courage to switch off the train set, the shadow of the man remained, a haunting specter etched into my very soul.

Terrified and filled with a newfound understanding of the darkness that surrounded me, I made the decision to abandon the train set altogether. I secretly buried it among unsuspecting boxes in the depth of my closet, hiding it away from prying eyes as if it were a cursed relic.

Months later, as I lay in bed on another sleepless night, I became acutely aware of the whispers that seemed to emanate from within the confines of my closet. The haunting words filled the air, whispering tales of forgotten souls and restless spirits, casting a chilling pall over my room. It was in that moment that the existence of ghosts became an undeniable reality in my young mind.

Years passed, and the memory of that eerie train set continued to linger, etched deeply into my consciousness. It served as a constant reminder that there are realms beyond our perception, where the normal intertwines with the paranormal, and where the shadows hold secrets that even the bravest among us dare not unveil.

REAL GHOST STORY

Haunted Hem

REAL GHOST STORY

Haunted Hem

I sat in the old, dimly lit room, the only source of light coming from the flickering candle on the dusty table beside me. The air was heavy, filled with the scent of old fabric and memories long gone. I couldn't help but feel a chill run down my spine as I stared at the ancient sewing machine in front of me, its tarnished metal and worn-out wood giving it an eerie appearance.

The memories of my mother's childhood best friend, Nancy, flooded my mind. I remembered the day my mom received the devastating call, the weight of the news visible on her face. Her expressions fell, and a deep sadness consumed her. She excused herself from the room, desperately trying to hide her pain, but I knew she couldn't contain her emotions for long. From the kitchen, I could hear her sobs echoing through the house, breaking my heart in the process.

As the days passed, we attended Nancy's funeral, saying our final goodbyes. It was a somber affair, filled with tears and long-held memories. And as the weekend came, we found ourselves at Nancy's house, surrounded by her grieving parents and husband. They were boxing up her belongings, a painful task that amplified the reality of her absence.

It was there, in the midst of the sorrowful scene, that my mom's eyes fell upon a sewing machine. It had caught her attention, as if pleading to be kept, to be cherished in Nancy's memory. My mom, always sentimental, asked if she could keep it, and to our surprise, Nancy's family agreed. I couldn't shake the feeling that there was something unusual about that sewing machine, something that went beyond mere sentimental value.

Nancy had been an incredibly talented seamstress, known for her craftsmanship and attention to detail. My mom often shared stories of her friend working tirelessly, creating intricate designs with every stitch.

To keep her memory alive, my mom started using the sewing machine, making garments and quilts, each one infused with Nancy's spirit.

It started out innocently enough. My mom taught me how to sew on that machine, guiding my hands as we worked on a quilt together. But then, something strange happened. The foot pedal got stuck, and yet, the machine continued to sew, as if guided by an unseen force. It effortlessly stitched until it reached the end of the row, stopping precisely where it should, without a hair's breadth of deviation. We exchanged bewildered glances, but brushed it off as a mere coincidence.

Days turned into weeks, and my mom's spin class became an opportunity for me to continue working on the quilt. But as I sat alone in that room with the haunted sewing machine, time seemed to play tricks on me. Minutes stretched into hours, yet the progress I made on the quilt felt like mere moments. It was disorienting, as if I had entered a distorted reality where the passage of time became a cruel joke.

When my mom returned from her exercise routine, she was amazed at how much I had accomplished. I had nearly finished half of the quilt, an impossible feat considering the limited time she was away. Yet, I couldn't shake the uneasy feeling that clung to the air, the sense that something otherworldly was at play beneath the surface.

Months passed, and I mustered the courage to confront the strange occurrences once more. It was a dark evening, the room illuminated only by the feeble light of a flickering candle. The shadows danced on the walls, creating eerie silhouettes that resembled a seamstress in motion. I felt a cold shiver crawl up my spine as I continued to work on the antique sewing machine, all alone in the room.

The sensation was undeniable, as if Nancy's presence lingered in the air, trying to communicate with me. I hurriedly ran to fetch my mom, desperate for her to witness the bizarre phenomenon. But as I returned, hope quickly turned to disappointment, for the shadows had vanished, leaving no trace of their ethereal existence.

That was the moment I decided to abandon the quilt, consumed by the fear and unease that the sewing machine had brought into our lives. My mom, sensing my discomfort, took it upon herself to finish the quilt, putting an end to the haunting project. I couldn't bear to use it, though, tucking it away in the depths of my closet, fearing the negative energy that seemed to be attached to it.

Was it Nancy's spirit, longing to be heard? Or was there something more sinister entwined within that antique sewing machine? I didn't dare ask my mom, afraid of her thinking I had gone mad. After all, how could I explain the unexplainable, the haunting presence that pervaded our lives?

To this day, my mom still has that sewing machine, a relic of the past and a reminder of the mysteries it holds. As for me, I keep my distance, wary of the unknown that resides within its creaking mechanisms. The quilt remains untouched, a silent reminder of the supernatural events that unfolded in our lives.

There are times when I catch glimpses of the quilt hidden away in the back of my closet, its colors muted and its patterns frozen in time. It serves as a constant reminder of the unexplained, a thread connecting me to the otherworldly presence that had infiltrated our lives.

I still wonder if it was merely Nancy's spirit reaching out, seeking solace in the world she once loved. Or perhaps, as the shadows danced and flickered in that dimly lit room, it was a force far more malevolent, lurking within the worn-out sewing machine, waiting for an unsuspecting victim to fall into its web.

Unresolved questions haunt my thoughts, and the fear

that something nefarious may have attached itself to that quilt lingers in the depths of my mind. It is a fear I cannot shake, a hesitation that keeps me from using or even facing the remnants of that haunting project.

The passage of time has not dulled the strange occurrences we experienced. Instead, it has deepened the mystery, leaving me with the unsettling realization that we had come face to face with something beyond the realm of the living. The sewing machine, once a treasure of nostalgia, has become a relic of the macabre, a whispered secret that only my mother and I share.

To this day, I dare not ask my mom if she too felt the chilling presence, if she witnessed the flickering shadows or sensed the disturbances in time. We have kept our shared secrets buried in the recesses of our hearts, protecting each other from the disbelieving eyes of the world.

As I sit here, recounting the events that unfolded in that eerie room, I can't help but wonder what became of Nancy's spirit, trapped or set free by the passing of time. Does she watch over us, her memories preserved in the stitches of that quilt? Or did she leave an imprint of her sorrow within that sewing machine, waiting for someone else to uncover the depths of its haunting power?

The truth remains elusive, hidden beneath layers of fear and fascination. I may never know the true origin of the mysterious occurrences that plagued us, the source of the shadows that danced on the walls, or the reason why time seemed to warp and twist when that antique sewing machine was in use.

All I can do is keep those memories locked away, an unsolved mystery forever etched in the fabric of our lives. And as I close the chapter on that haunting experience, I can't help but feel a lingering sense of dread whenever I pass by my mom's sewing room, where the enigmatic machine sits, waiting, silent yet full of secrets.

REAL GHOST STORY

Phantom Playthings

I sat in the dimly lit room, the soft glow of the moon peeking through the curtains, I couldn't help but feel a sense of unease. My gaze was fixated on the old dollhouse in the corner, its vintage furniture casting eerie shadows on the walls. It had been a few weeks since my 10th birthday, the day I received this long-awaited gift. The moment my father had brought it up to my room, a rush of excitement had flooded my veins.

The dollhouse stood there, its presence like a silent

sentinel, beckoning me to explore its secrets. The figures and furniture that came with it added to its charm, their delicate features frozen in time. I couldn't resist but imagine the stories they had to tell, the adventures that awaited within those miniature walls.

My father, sensing my joy, granted me an extra 30 minutes to play even though it was already my bedtime. I rubbed my tired eyes, a combination of exhaustion and anticipation. With a deep breath, I dove into the world of make-believe.

The minutes turned into hours as I lost myself in the intricate details of the dollhouse. But as I prepared to close up the dollhouse, a chilling sight caught my attention. Through one of the exquisitely crafted windows, a shadow passed by. It couldn't be, I thought. Against my wall, there was no room for such eerie figures to exist. Curiosity gnawed at me, and I ventured to the back of the dollhouse, only to find nothing that could have caused that unsettling shadow.

As time went by, the memory of the strange incident was pushed to the back of my mind. I reveled in the joy the dollhouse brought me, unaware of the haunting experiences it would soon deliver. One cold, rainy day, as I escaped the monotony of school and the gloominess of the weather, I had sought solace in the dollhouse. But when I opened its tiny doors, an unnerving feeling washed over me. The figures and furniture were no longer where I had carefully arranged them the day before. Anger surged through me, suspecting a prank from my father.

I stormed downstairs, arms crossed, straight into my father's office. He looked up, his eyes behind his glasses reflecting confusion. I demanded to know why he had moved my dolls, my voice betraying my frustration. He stared at me, blinking, clearly unaware of what I was talking about. "What do you mean?" he asked, genuinely puzzled. Frustration bubbled within me as I repeated my question, emphasizing the importance of not moving my dolls without permission. I stormed out of the room, leaving him behind, trying to piece together what had just transpired. Did he not realize how much I cherished this gift? How could he think I would be careless with my dolls?

As I ascended the staircase, anger still coursing through my veins, a whisper drifted through the air, barely audible. It called my name, but it was not my father's voice. It was a woman's voice, soft and distant. I froze on the stairs, my heart pounding in my chest. The whisper came and went, leaving me both intrigued and terrified. I tried to shrug it off, attributing it to my overactive imagination playing tricks on me.

Dinner that evening had an unsettling atmosphere. The tension between my father and me lingered, my arms crossed as a silent protest. I pushed my food around on the plate, making it clear that I wouldn't be appeased easily. Enough was enough, my father snapped. "I didn't touch your dolls," he stated matter-of-factly, his words muffled by the food in his mouth. I dropped my fork, finding some satisfaction in the fact that I had made my point, but his answer did nothing to ease my troubled mind.

"Then who did?" I muttered under my breath, my frustration laced with genuine curiosity. His response was nonchalant; he suggested that perhaps I had forgotten how I had arranged the dolls. I rolled my eyes at his dismissive remark, knowing that I would never make such a careless mistake. As I made my way back upstairs, I couldn't shake the feeling that something else was at play. Just when I thought it couldn't get any stranger, the unseen whispers returned, calling my name, taunting me with their ethereal presence.

Night after night, my dreams became engulfed in darkness and terror. The nightmares rendered me helpless, trapped in a bathtub, water cascading upon me, suds covering my face. A cold hand pressed against my back, forcing me down into the water, drowning me. Each time I jolted awake, gasping for air, the image of my dead mother haunting my thoughts. It was a torment I couldn't escape.

But it wasn't just the nightmares that plagued me. In the dead of the night, the room filled with an eerie silence, I would hear ghostly footsteps echoing through the room. The sound seemed to originate from the dollhouse, yet no visible source could be found. My heart raced as I lay there in bed, paralyzed with fear. The dark presence that seemed to emanate from the dollhouse was suffocating, leaving me longing for the light and a sense of safety.

Unable to bear the constant torment, I finally mustered the courage to approach my father about the strange occurrences. As we sat at the dinner table one evening, my hands trembling, I decided to share my secret. With a hesitant voice, I confessed the vivid nightmares, the unsettling whispers, and the inexplicable footsteps that haunted me every night.

My father's face turned pale, his fork mid-air, frozen in disbelief. He stared at the table, his eyes distant, lost in a memory he had tried to bury. It was only after some prodding and a hint of desperation in my voice that he finally opened up about the dollhouse's tragic past.

He revealed that the dollhouse had been a gift from a friend, whose sister had endured a harrowing tragedy. She had drowned her own two children in a bathtub before taking her own life. My father's friend, burdened by the dark history of the dollhouse, had sought solace in its removal from his life. It was then that he had asked my father if he would want the dollhouse for me, unaware of the haunting presence it carried.

I sat there, stunned. The dollhouse that I had once cherished was now tainted by a dark and chilling tale. My father's decision to remove it from our lives soon afterward was a mixture of protection and relief. Part of me mourned the loss, as I had grown fond of those miniature walls and the world they contained, but the eerie vibes and the horrors they had brought into my dreams were overwhelming.

As I grew older, my curiosity about the dollhouse and its haunting past lingered. I often found myself reflecting on the nightmares that had plagued me and the whispers that had echoed through the house. It was a chilling reminder of the supernatural forces that exist beyond our comprehension.

I sought solace in researching paranormal phenomena, drawn to stories of haunted objects and the people who dared to uncover their secrets. While I couldn't definitively prove that the dollhouse was haunted, the harrowing experiences I had endured left little room for doubt in my mind.

Years passed, but the memory of the dollhouse and its haunting presence remained etched in my mind. It served as a reminder of the unexplained mysteries that hide in the darkest corners of our existence. The incident had left an indelible mark on my psyche, shaping my fascination with the unknown and fueling my desire to explore the supernatural.

To this day, the question of whether the dollhouse was truly haunted remains unanswered. But for me, the nightmares, the whispers, and the unexplainable footsteps that still echo in the recesses of my memory are evidence enough. The dollhouse served as a portal to a realm I never thought existed, a portal that forever changed the way I viewed the world around me.

And so, I continue my journey, embracing the mysteries that lie in wait, ready to unearth the truth behind the inexplicable. The dollhouse may be gone, but its haunting legacy lives on, a reminder of the darkness that lurks in the most unexpected places.

REAL GHOST STORY

Sinister Satchel

REAL GHOST STORY

Sinister Satchel

I stood at the entrance of my childhood bedroom, nostalgia consuming me as I glanced at the few belongings I had taken from my late brother. Halloween 2012 had changed everything for us. That fateful night, a home invasion had robbed me of my beloved sibling, who had only recently moved into his own apartment. Still raw with grief, I clung to his memory by keeping a few of his possessions close to my heart.

Among these mementos was a mysterious suitcase. I

couldn't explain why I chose to keep it, particularly since it seemed utterly insane. A haunted suitcase? It sounded ludicrous even to my own ears. Nevertheless, I believed that this enigmatic item held a supernatural presence. I had requested it with the intention of using it when I ventured off to college after high school graduation.

At first, when I brought the suitcase home, I failed to notice anything peculiar. Perhaps it was due to my overwhelming sorrow, the weight of loss enveloping my spirit. But it wasn't long before strange occurrences began to unfold. Unexplained mood swings would plague me, as though an invisible force tugged at my emotions, leaving me in a constant state of unease and anxiety. I confided in my parents, and they took me to a doctor who prescribed antidepressants. But the pills were powerless against the unsettling sensations that invaded me.

One day, while organizing my closet, I placed the haunted suitcase near my television stand. Almost instantly, the television began to malfunction, its screen glitching and picture freezing. It was a logical explanation, one that I readily accepted in my grief-stricken state. But as time passed, my skepticism waned.

A particularly desolate night, overcome with yearning

for my lost brother, I unzipped the haunted suitcase. Filled with the scent of his essence, it was as if his spirit still lingered within its confines. Lost in my own melancholy, a picture hanging on the wall above my bed suddenly plummeted to the floor, shattering into countless pieces. It startled me, the sound echoing through the silence, and I couldn't dismiss it as mere happenstance any longer.

From that moment on, my nights took a sinister turn. Like clockwork, I would awaken at the stroke of three, a haunting hour when the veil between the living and the dead thins. The oppressive feeling of being watched consumed me, suffocating the air in my room. I searched desperately for any sign of an intruder but found no one.

Then, in the depths of one sleepless night, as I lay in bed, I felt a chilling breath against my cheek. The strands of my hair danced in time to this ethereal exhalation, and terror gripped my heart. I bolted out of bed, racing to seek solace in my parents' room, my pulse racing in my ears.

Determined to uncover the truth, I devised a plan. I moved the haunted suitcase up to the attic, banishing it from my daily existence. To my amazement, the nightmares ceased, the anxiety lifted, and the pervasive dread dissipated. It was as if the malevolent presence attached to the suitcase had been exorcised from my life.

Do I believe my brother's spirit haunted that suitcase? The answer eludes me. All I know is that some supernatural entity had attached itself to the cursed object, haunting me mercilessly. And now, as it languishes in the darkness of my parents' attic, my life has found a semblance of peace once more.

The haunting presence of the suitcase served as a grim reminder of the horrors that can lurk beneath the surface of our material possessions. It was a lesson in the unexplainable, a testament to the unending mysteries of the unknown. And as I embark on my journey beyond the confines of my childhood home, I carry with me the memory of that haunting experience, a chilling reminder that not all that we inherit holds salvation, but instead, may be a gateway to a darker realm.

A PARANORMAL THRILLER

THE DARK TRUTH

....

EVE S EVANS

COMING FALL 2023

PROLOGUE

Megan's rapid breathing filled the house as she clutched the phone to her ear. "911. Can you please state the address of your emergency?" the operator's voice pierced through her muddled thoughts. Megan's lips quivered, and she struggled to form words. Panic consumed her as her mind raced to recall the address. She let out a breathless, panicked murmur, "I… Um…"

"Ma'am? Hello? What is the address?" The operator's voice was stern.

"H-Hold on. I can't think. Let me just… let me find it." Megan's heart pounded as she stumbled into the hallway. She tried not to look at the blood, but it was everywhere, seeping into the edges of her vision no matter where she looked. Her hands trembled as she clutched at the wall for support.

"What is your name, ma'am?" the operator asked, trying to keep her on the line.

"Megan Emmerson," she answered, her voice barely above a whisper. "G-give me a minute… I think… I almost got it."

As Megan stepped into the dimly lit foyer, her eyes immediately landed on the stack of old mail resting on the sideboard. Without hesitation, she reached out and snatched the top envelope, her fingers fumbling over the paper as she read the address out loud. "I've found it. 2377 W Tarvish Drive," she murmured, her breath hitching in her chest.

The 911 dispatcher's voice crackled through the phone, breaking through the silence. "Is that in Brooktown?" she asked, the question echoing in Megan's ear.

Megan nodded, even though the dispatcher couldn't see her. "Y-yes," she stammered, her voice trembling with fear.

The dispatcher's voice was calm and measured, a stark contrast to Megan's frantic state. "Can you tell me what's going on there? What's the nature of the emergency?"

Megan's mind raced as she tried to form a coherent response. She glanced down at her hands and her eyes widened at the sight of the blood staining her palms. "There's...there's a lot of blood," she managed to choke out, her vision blurred with tears.

"Is someone hurt? Do you know what happened?" the dispatcher pressed, her voice growing more urgent.

Megan took a deep breath, trying to steady her nerves. "I...I don't know," she confessed, her voice shaking. "I don't know where Carol is."

The dispatcher's voice was filled with concern. "Who's Carol?"

Megan's heart pounded in her chest as she struggled to find the words to describe her friend. "She is...she was the homeowner," she explained, her voice barely above a whisper. "I was supposed to meet her here, but...but something is wrong. Something is really wrong."

As she spoke, Megan's eyes darted around the room, searching for any sign of Carol. But all she could see was the blood, the crimson stains marring the once pristine walls and floor. Her stomach churned as she realized the magnitude of the situation.

The dispatcher's voice was cool and collected, lacking any hint of emotion. "Who is Carol?" she inquired. Megan felt a pang of annoyance at the dispatcher's nonchalant tone.

Ignoring the question, Megan braced herself against the wall, trying to steady her trembling legs. She needed to focus on something other than the horror painted before her eyes. "Are you sending someone?" she asked instead.

The dispatcher's response was matter-of-fact, almost robotic. "Yes, police and emergency services are already on the way," she informed Megan. "Answering my questions isn't going to hinder responders. I just need to ask so that I know what is going on and can relay any important information to the responders."

Megan took a deep, shuddering breath. "O-okay, I see," she stuttered.

"Is this your house?" the dispatcher continued.

"No," Megan replied, her voice barely above a whisper. "No, it is Carol and Jim's."

There was a brief pause on the other end of the line, and Megan could hear the sound of fingers typing on a keyboard. "Who are Carol and Jim?" the dispatcher asked.

As Megan spoke, tears streamed down her face, and her voice trembled with fear and grief. She took a deep breath before continuing, "Carol is my best friend. Jim, well, he is...her husband," she paused, choking up on his name, her throat clenching. "Jim is dead."

There was a brief, stunned silence on the other end of the line, and Megan could hear the dispatcher shuffling papers before she regained her composure. "Jim is dead? Are you certain?"

Megan's hands shook as she clutched the phone tightly. "Yes, I am sure. He is dead."

The dispatcher's voice was calm and steady. "What happened, Megan?"

"I have no idea," Megan sobbed, her body shaking with sobs. "I came over to see Carol and found the front door ajar. I tried calling out but nobody answered, so I went inside. And then I saw the blood. All over the wall, some on the floor. There's a bloody shirt too."

"Do you know who the blood belongs to?" the dispatcher asked.

"I think it's Carol's, but I can't find her. She's not here."

"Okay, and how do you know Jim is dead? Where is he?"

"When I was walking around, looking for them, I went into the office. That's where I found him." Megan's voice was barely above a whisper now.

"Are you sure Jim isn't breathing? Did you check for a pulse?"

Megan's hands shook as she clutched her phone, her eyes squeezed shut. She couldn't erase the image of Jim's bloody face from her mind. "No, Jim's not alive. He's missing half of his face," she whispered, her voice breaking.

There was a long pause on the other end of the line before the dispatcher spoke again. "I see."

"Are the police arriving?"

Megan's heart pounded in her chest as she strained to hear the approaching sirens in the distance. "Yes, I think so. I hear sirens."

The dispatcher's voice was calm but urgent. "Alright, Megan, I need you to walk outside. You can keep me on the line if you'd like, but I need you to come out with your hands up so that the police know you aren't a threat. Can you do that?"

Megan stared at the door in front of her. She could hear the sirens growing louder by the second. "Y-yes," she stammered, trying to steady her breathing.

"Good. Let me know when you're with the officers," the dispatcher instructed.

Megan took a deep breath and slowly pushed away from the wall steadying her. She made her way to the front door, her hand shaking as she reached for the handle. She took another deep breath before pulling the door open and stepping out onto the porch.

The sound of the sirens was almost deafening now, and Megan could see flashing lights in the distance. "I'm outside," she said, her voice barely above a whisper.

"Good," the dispatcher replied. "Just stay calm and keep your hands up until the officers get to you."

An officer appeared in front of Megan, his hand resting on his gun. Megan took a step back, her heart in her throat. The officer's expression was guarded until he saw that she wasn't carrying a weapon. "Did you call it in?" he asked, his tone demanding an answer.

Megan nodded, holding out her phone to show him the 911 call. "I have an officer with me," she told the dispatcher, her voice shaking despite her efforts to remain calm.

"Okay, Megan, I'm going to let you go now," the dispatcher said.

Megan lowered the phone, her hands trembling. She couldn't believe what she had just witnessed. The officer was speaking to her, but she couldn't make out his words. Before she knew it, her knees buckled, and she fell to the ground, the phone slipping from her grasp. Sobs wracked her body as the reality of the situation hit her like a ton of bricks. Jim was dead, and her best friend was probably gone too. "No," she sobbed, her voice barely above a whisper. "No, no, no."

1

As Julie, Seth, and Lillian made their way up the gravel path leading to the Victorian house, the sound of each crunching step echoed through the quiet, small neighborhood. Julie felt the cool breeze on her face and paused for a moment to look up at the grandiose façade of the house. The exterior was made of grey brick, with intricate white woodwork adorning the edges of the windows and doors. The front porch was supported by pillars that seemed to rise up to the sky, and a large window with stained glass sat above the door.

Julie noticed that once they had approached the small subdivision on the drive in, a row of cherry blossom trees lined the street, their delicate pink petals fluttering in the breeze. The trees seemed to be a stark contrast to the otherwise eerie atmosphere of the area.

The subdivision itself was comprised of a few scattered

small, identical houses, each with its own picket fence and meticulously maintained lawn. The homes seemed as if they hadn't been updated or changed in decades. The picket fences were pristine white, and the lawns were perfectly trimmed and edged.

Despite the manicured appearance of the homes and landscapes, there was an eerie feeling that permeated the air. The silence was deafening, with no sounds of children playing or dogs barking. It was as if the entire subdivision was frozen in a state of perpetual stillness.

The air smelled fresher than the city, with a hint of pine mixed with the sweet aroma of cherry blossoms. It was a soothing scent, but it only added to the eerie feeling of the area. It was almost as if the sweet smell was masking something sinister lurking just beneath the surface.

Seth stopped in his tracks just before the front door, positioning himself behind Julie. He took a moment to survey the yard, drinking in every detail of their new home. His eyes scanned the area, lingering on the picket fence that enclosed the perimeter of the yard, the rose bushes that adorned the wooden slats, and the lush, green grass that appeared to be without fault. He found it peculiar that a home that had been uninhabited for so long could be in such pristine condition.

Suddenly, a mixture of scents wafted towards him on the breeze, instantly calming his apprehension and melting away any fears he had. The sweet aroma of cherry blossoms mingled with the heady fragrance of roses, and the faint scent of pine added a touch of freshness to the air.

"Ready?" Seth asked as he placed a hand on Julie's elbow from behind.

"As ready as I'll ever be," Julie turned to glance back at him and shot him a nervous smile.

Julie took a deep breath and gripped the key tightly in her hand, feeling a sense of trepidation wash over her. This wasn't just any new house; it was another potential murder house waiting to be explored. As she stepped up to the front door, she couldn't help but wonder what secrets it was hiding, what dark history lay behind its walls.

This had become Julie's life ever since her first book, Missing in the Everglades, became a bestseller. She had traveled from one murder house to another, living in each one until she uncovered its secrets and recorded them in writing. It was a thrilling and dangerous career, but it was what she loved to do.

With a shaking hand, Julie inserted the key into the lock and turned it. The door creaked open, and she couldn't help but feel a sense of excitement mixed with trepidation. The Victorian house loomed before them, its creaky boards and musty smell giving it an eerie undertone.

Julie took a deep breath and turned to Seth and Lillian, who were following closely behind her. Seth's tall and broad figure towered over her, and his dark hair and piercing blue eyes only added to his rugged good looks. Despite the gruesome nature of her job, he always managed to keep a calm and steady demeanor, a trait that she admired about him.

Julie heard the clinking and rattling of the contents of the cardboard box that Seth held in his arms as he shifted his feet. Beside them walked Lillian, who, at eight years old, bore a striking resemblance to Seth, with her bright blue eyes and blonde hair. Because of her young age and innocence, Julie was determined to shield her from the harsh reality of her work in true crime. Lillian skipped along, unaware of the dark history of the houses they moved into. Julie struggled to strike a delicate balance between pursuing her passion and protecting her family from the horrors that came with it.

As they stood at the threshold of the new house, Seth's tanned skin and bright blue eyes caught Julie's attention. His brown hair was slicked back with gel, highlighting his chiseled jawline and making him look exceptionally handsome.

Julie couldn't help but notice the faint bulge of muscles under Seth's white shirt and the bead of sweat that seeped through the fabric, a testament to his dedication to staying fit at 43. As a writer, she felt self-conscious next to him. Julie spent most of her time hunched over a computer, writing for hours on end to complete each new true crime thriller as quickly as possible. Her skin was paler than Seth's, a sign of her lack of outdoor activity. Her slender frame seemed almost fragile compared to his toned physique.

Despite her physical limitations, Julie had her own way of immersing herself in her writing. She often chose to stay in murder houses to get a real feel for the place. However, she never wanted to stay longer than necessary.

The darkness and the ghosts of the past had always seemed to seep into Julie's soul, leaving her drained and haunted long after she left. As she adjusted her blonde weave, Julie felt a sense of excitement mixed with apprehension. It wasn't just the new house that was making her heart race, but the thrill of the unknown and the sense of adventure that came with exploring each new place they lived in. Her daughter Lillian was just as eager, always the adventurous one in their family with a fearless spirit inherited from her father.

Lillian practically bounced with excitement, her eyes sparkling with anticipation. "What are you waiting for, mommy? Let's go in!" she exclaimed, tugging on the sleeve of Julie's jacket.

Julie couldn't help but smile at Lillian's infectious energy. She ruffled Lillian's blonde hair and took a deep breath before she stepped through the threshold and into the house's foyer. The house had been opened up since the tragedy that had occurred there, but Julie still felt a sense of unease.

Lillian's eyes widened as she stepped inside their new home, taking in every inch of the spacious entranceway.

She spun in circles, her long hair flying around like a whirlwind, and let out a soft gasp of awe.

"Wow," she breathed, her voice barely above a whisper. "This place is so cool."

Julie chuckled softly at Lillian's excitement, watching as she rushed past her and stopped in the middle of the hallway. A gold-rimmed mirror caught Lillian's eye, and she walked over to it, brushing away the cobwebs that clung to the frame.

Lillian pointed at the dusty old table runner draped over a sideboard and expressed her admiration for its age.

Continuing to explore the space, Seth and Julie began unloading boxes from the car. Seth stretched his back with a groan as he set down a heavy box. "I'll put everything here for now," he said, nodding at the growing pile of boxes. "You go ahead and look around."

Julie hesitated for a moment, her lower lip between her teeth. "Are you sure?" she asked, furrowing her brow with concern.

Seth nodded, his eyes determined. "Don't worry about me. I'll take care of it. You go and explore our new home."

Julie smiled gratefully before turning to follow Lillian. Walking through the hallway, she noticed the high ceiling and dark wooden rafters, strung with cobwebs. There was so much character in this place, Julie couldn't wait to uncover every hidden detail.

Just as Julie left Seth to the boxes, Lillian wasted no time in declaring her intentions. "I'm gonna go pick a room," she announced, her voice filled with excitement as she took off running up the stairs. Julie watched her go, amused by her eagerness.

She took a moment to absorb her new surroundings. The front door led directly to a landing, with a staircase leading up to the second floor. Without hesitation, she began to wander around the ground floor, taking in the details. The flooring was a warm shade of brown hardwood, with some areas slightly faded from years of sun exposure. The walls were painted a soft cream color, which only served to enhance the natural light that flooded the space. As she continued to explore, she couldn't help but feel a sense of excitement and anticipation building inside her.

Julie's eyes wandered around the spacious hallway, soaking in the pristine white walls and the polished hardwood floors that gleamed under the soft glow of the chandelier. Her attention was immediately drawn to the left, where a white door with a gleaming gold handle caught her eye. Without hesitation, she pushed it open, and her jaw dropped at the sight before her. The spacious bathroom was a masterpiece of luxury and comfort, with its large oval-shaped bathtub taking center stage. She couldn't resist the temptation to run her fingers over the smooth porcelain surface, imagining herself sinking into the warm, bubbly water after a long day of writing. The thought of the air filled with steam, the aroma of lavender candles, and a glass of wine in hand, made her smile with anticipation.

As Julie took in the opulence of the room, she couldn't help but reminisce of their last place, where they had to make do with a small tub. This new bathtub was definitely a luxurious upgrade, and she could already picture herself spending hours soaking in it, lost in a world of relaxation and peace.

Julie stepped out of the bathroom and made her way down the hallway. At the end of the corridor, she spotted the first door on the right, and she couldn't resist the urge to peek inside. As she turned the handle, she was met with a spacious kitchen that took her breath away. The modern white fixtures caught her eye, and she couldn't help but feel a sense of pride that this sleek space was now hers. The big windows overlooking the backyard flooded the room with natural light, making everything look even more inviting. In the center of the room, an island beckoned Julie with four tall stools set around it, inviting her to sit and bask in the ambiance of her new home. Beyond the island, a larger dining table stood proud, its wooden surface gleaming beneath the sun's rays. Julie could already picture herself hosting dinner parties in this space, surrounded by friends and family, enjoying the fruits of her labor.

As Julie took in the details of the kitchen, she noticed the white granite counters that lined the walls, complemented by the matching grey fixtures on the stools. The cupboards next to the sink were a light grey with silver handles, and she made a mental note to organize her new dishes and cookware in there.

Julie paused at the sink, admiring the pristine white ceramic basin before looking down at the taps. They were a little rusted, and she made a mental note to give them a decent scrub later.

As she wandered around the kitchen, she couldn't help but daydream about the memories they would create there. The unfamiliar layout had been a puzzle to solve, but she felt confident that with time, it would become a comfortable and functional space for their family of three.

Her mind drifted to their daily ritual of gathering around the table for meals, and she smiled as she pictured them in that open, airy kitchen. She envisioned her daughter Lillian perched on a stool at the sleek counter, her curly hair bouncing as she eagerly dug into a plate of fluffy pancakes drenched in syrup.

Meanwhile, Julie's husband Seth was bustling around the stove, expertly flipping eggs and bacon, and fussing over his beloved cup of coffee. Although the kitchen was far from familiar, Julie could already feel the warmth and love that would fill it as they made it their own. She exited the kitchen with the vision of their family still in her mind.

As Julie stepped into the living room of their new house, she was struck by the emptiness of the space. The room felt almost haunted, with most of the furniture having been removed after an incident that had occurred there. All that remained was an old leather recliner, worn and cracked, and a tattered red rug that looked like it had been through a war. The walls were bare, and the floorboards creaked under her feet, adding to the eerie atmosphere.

Looking around, Julie couldn't help but feel like something was missing in the room, something that should have been there but wasn't. It was like the room was waiting for something to fill it up and give it a purpose. She knew that once they got their own furniture in there, it would feel less empty and more like a home.

Julie decided to leave the living room for the time being

and explore the rest of the house. As she turned to face the hallway, she felt a strange pull in her stomach, as if something was calling her. She followed the pull to the end of the hallway, where a door was tucked away behind the back of the staircase. It was closed, and as she reached for the handle, she felt a strange resistance, like something was pushing back against her hand, preventing her from opening the door. She pulled harder, but the door remained shut.

With a determined grip on the door handle, Julie put all her weight into turning it, hoping to gain access. The mechanism resisted at first, but after a few more attempts, it finally gave way with a shudder, and the door released. She stumbled inside, caught off guard by the sudden release of resistance, and almost lost her balance. Blinking rapidly to adjust her eyes to the dimness, she took in her surroundings. The curtains were drawn halfway, casting a murky light over the room, and she caught a glimpse of grey blinds behind them. The air was stale, heavy with the weight of unspoken secrets and unshed tears. She paused and took a deep breath, trying to steady herself. This was where it had happened, where the tragedy had unfolded.

Julie knew every inch of that room, having studied photos of it for hours before coming there. It was the office, the room where Jim had taken his own life after murdering his wife.

Please remember to leave a review after reading.

AVAILABLE ON ALL PODCAST NETWORKS

CHECK OUT
— PODCASTS —
HOSTED BY EVE:

TRUE WHISPERS
A TRUE CRIME PODCAST

A TRULY HAUNTED PODCAST
A PARANORMAL PODCAST

FOREVER HAUNTED
A PARANORMAL PODCAST

BONE CHILLING TALES
A PARANORMAL PODCAST

THE GHOST THAT HAUNTS ME
A PARANORMAL PODCAST

FIND EVE
— ON —
YOUTUBE:

 DARK ABYSS

 eves.evansauthor

 Eve S Evans Author

 author_eve_evans
TikTok

For exclusive deals, ARCs, and giveaways!

If you love to review books and would like a chance to snatch up one of Eve's ARCs before publication, follow her facebook page or TikTok.

ABOUT
—— THE ——
AUTHOR

Since my first publication to the present day in 2023, I have gained a wealth of knowledge about life and my exploration of the paranormal. My journey started several years ago when I lived in various haunted houses. However, it was one particular house that left me feeling drained and exhausted. Desperate for answers, I embarked on a mission to interview numerous individuals who have also experienced hauntings, regardless of their profession or background.

But what have I learned from this journey so far? I'm uncertain if I'll ever obtain the answers I seek in this lifetime. Nonetheless, I'm determined to persist in my pursuit of knowledge by conducting interviews and engaging in ghost hunting activities. I'm committed to uncovering as many answers as possible before I too become a ghost.

This year, I have a number of books scheduled for

release and I am widely recognized for my compilations of "real ghost stories". However, I have decided to challenge myself by writing mostly fictional works centered around haunted houses. If you're interested in reading one of my anthologies, I recommend starting with "True Ghost Stories of First Responders", where I interview police officers, firefighters, 911 dispatchers, and other professionals who share their eeriest calls that could be considered "ghostly".

In addition, I am looking forward to publishing my paranormal memoir this year. I aspire to reveal my personal journey and experiences to readers. Until then, I want to reassure those who may be fearful or feel like they are experiencing inexplicable phenomena in their homes that they are not alone. I have been there too, and I know it can be overwhelming.

If you need someone to talk to about what you're experiencing but don't know where to turn, you can message me on Instagram or Facebook.

November 2023:

Paranormal Objects

Haunted Asylums

December 2023:

Haunted Hotels

Haunted Islands

January 2024:

My Haunted House: Volume 2

February 2024:

Paranormal Places 2

March 2024:

Haunted Farms

Printed in Dunstable, United Kingdom

65145490R00088